The H ... As well as books for ... poetry, and has had poems p ... hologies for younger readers. He p ... The Poetry Roadshow, an entertainment for ... ols. Roger was trained as a fine artist and taught art and CDT in secondary and middle schools for fifteen years before moving into junior education. He currently teaches music one day a week in a primary school. He is the leader of a popular rock band and one half of an alternative comedy duo. He also runs a successful network marketing business. Roger Stevens lives and works in Kent.

THE HOWEN

Roger Stevens

PUFFIN BOOKS

For Paul and Kate

With special thanks for their invaluable help to the children, Jackie, Hazel, Maureen, GMY and Ken, to the grown-up, Thomas Callaghan, and to Jill.

PUFFIN BOOKS

Published by the Penguin Group
Penguin Books Ltd, 27 Wrights Lane, London W8 5TZ, England
Penguin Books USA Inc., 375 Hudson Street, New York, New York 10014, USA
Penguin Books Australia Ltd, Ringwood, Victoria, Australia
Penguin Books Canada Ltd, 10 Alcorn Avenue, Toronto, Ontario, Canada M4V 3B2
Penguin Books (NZ) Ltd, 182–190 Wairau Road, Auckland 10, New Zealand

Penguin Books Ltd, Registered Offices: Harmondsworth, Middlesex, England

First published by Viking 1993
Published in Puffin Books 1996
1 3 5 7 9 10 8 6 4 2

Copyright © Roger Stevens, 1993
All rights reserved

The moral right of the author has been asserted

Made and printed in England by Clays Ltd, St Ives plc

CONTENTS

1	THE ATTIC	1
2	THE BRETHREN	13
3	THE REBELS	21
4	THE PROWLER	32
5	CAPTURED	42
6	BETRAYED	52
7	BREAKFAST	64
8	REUNION	73
9	IN THE DARK	82
10	FIRE	90
11	THE CHUTE	104
12	SMOKE	114
13	THE WEB	125
14	THE KEY	137
15	WELCOME	145
16	DOG-TIRED	162

— listen; there's a hell
of a good universe next door; let's go

e.e. cummings

CHAPTER I

THE ATTIC

Summer was already a distant memory. The cracked grey concrete playground was a cold and draughty place. Some of the older pupils were rushing about playing Killer but most of the children huddled together in little groups, trying to hide from the freezing wind in the shelter of the red-brick outbuildings.

A rat bolted out of the school door chased by Mad Max, the Head's dog, a scrawny terrier rescued from Battersea Dogs' Home. The pair scurried in and out of the scaffolding poles which clung precariously to the east end of the building like a geometric web of grey metal tubing. Max was barking furiously all the time, egged on by cries of encouragement from the children; the rat made no sound at all.

Mrs Wisbech, known to all as the Witch, came running over as the children gathered round the builders' skips, waving, laughing, yelling at the dog. The rat had long gone, of course, but Max was determined to keep the chase alive and was barking and growling at a pile of bricks.

Mrs Wisbech was flustered, hunting in the folds of

her coat for her whistle. The children knew they weren't allowed in this part of the playground, they'd been told over and over that it wasn't safe. Well, she'd send them back in to work. That was where they should be. Kids had plenty of time to play at home; school was for learning. The Witch, of course, was not a very popular teacher.

An old, skinny magpie alighted on the ancient school clock tower and surveyed the commotion below. It puffed up its feathers against the biting cold. Winter was early this year and this one would probably be the magpie's last.

The clock's single hand said twenty past something – just as it had since any pupil or member of staff could remember, even old Stick, the caretaker, who had been at the school since the Ice Age. Like the clock, the main school building was very old: pre-Victorian. Nobody seemed to know what it had been before it was a school. Narrow corridors twisted and turned around poky, poorly-heated classrooms. Rusty plumbing hissed and belched. The school had been condemned thirty years ago but only now, after the recent near-hurricane winds, had the axe finally fallen. The east end of the building had been declared unsafe and next term everyone was being moved to a much bigger secondary school, five kilometres away.

While the dog was chasing the rat and the Witch was hunting for her whistle, Diz and Sharon were winning a game of Killer, a type of hide and seek on the run. But they were fast running out of places to hide. They crouched near the scaffolding in search of a new bolthole, looking round anxiously, for the cries of their pursuers were getting louder by the second. Diz caught sight of the magpie as it rose gracefully from the clock tower, cutting an arc across the northerly wind and disappearing into the gloomy sky.

'One for sorrow,' he said, half to himself. 'But at least the bird's free.'

Diz pushed his hands deeper into the pockets of his jacket and shivered from the cold. He hated being cooped up in school. The only lesson he enjoyed was Computer Studies – and that was only once a week for one term. After Christmas he would have to do Drama – and after that Home Economics. At least they'd be at the new school by then.

Sharon, his sister, grabbed his arm. 'Quick! Where now?' There seemed to be no escape. Then Diz had a bright idea. 'In there, the DT room!'

'We're not allowed in there and anyway, it'll be locked,' Sharon retorted.

Diz ducked under the orange tape that warned pupils to keep away and tried the door. It opened. Sharon followed him quickly into the building and they slammed the door shut. Silence greeted them. It was cold inside and the familiar smells of wood, varnish and glue were sharpened by newer notes of dampness and neglect.

'There,' grinned Diz, 'it was open. I told you.'

'We'll get into trouble being here. You know it's out of bounds,' Sharon began, as Diz put his finger to his lips. 'Shh.'

They could hear their pursuers outside, arguing about where to look next. The doorknob turned. Sharon and Diz crouched behind a bench and held their breath. They felt a gust of icy air around their legs as the door opened but none of their friends came in and the door was quickly closed again.

'I think that was Baxter,' Diz said in a low voice. 'He wouldn't risk being caught in here with the Witch on patrol!'

The whistle finally blew. 'We'd better go,' Diz whispered.

'No, let's wait a few minutes. We don't want anyone to see us coming out of here, do we? What have you got next?'

'Old Nick for English.'

'That's all right, then. He's always late.'

They stood up. Diz stretched and yawned. He was small for his age. His sister was a year younger than he but she was the same height and they were often mistaken for twins. They both had their father's looks – thick, light-brown hair and large, grey eyes, a full mouth set in a round, friendly face and what their mum called a generous nose.

For a brother and sister they got on well enough. Sharon thought Diz was impulsive and stubborn. Diz thought Sharon was clever but bossy. And although they were in different years they often went around together at school. They did the shopping for their mum on Saturdays because she had to work six days a week and they went for long bike rides together to get away from the house. They were good friends, except indoors at home, when they seemed to fight most of the time over who watched what on television. Sharon followed the soaps. Diz hated them. He preferred adventures and cartoons.

Sharon made her way to the teacher's desk. It was

strange to see the Design and Technology room clean and tidy. Usually the floor was covered in wood shavings and tools were left lying around. She picked up a pink folder from a tall pile of dusty papers on the desk and started leafing through it.

'I wonder if there are any exam papers here,' Sharon said.

Diz was toying with what looked like a large wonky crane. It was made, rather badly, of wood and plastic tubes. But before he could tell his sister not to be so stupid they heard voices outside: teachers' voices.

'It's the Witch, talking to the Head. What's he doing here?' Diz whispered in alarm. Nobody ever saw the Head around the school. When he wasn't drinking tea in his room he was away at a meeting or on a course. 'I think they're coming in.'

They looked round desperately for somewhere to hide.

'Oh no,' said Diz, 'if we're caught in here we'll get done. We'll probably be expelled.'

'You always go over the top, Diz,' said Sharon. 'The worst we'll get is a detention.' She looked round. 'Quick, let's try the woodstore.'

The store was through a big red door at the back of the DT room. It was usually kept locked, but unexpectedly the door opened and they slipped through, closing it quietly behind them. A close shave. The voices of the teachers could now be heard coming into the classroom. Sharon and Diz crouched down in the dusty darkness, hardly daring to breathe.

'No, there's nobody here,' the Head was saying. 'You must have been mistaken.'

They were talking right outside the storeroom door.

'And while we're on the subject,' Mrs Wisbech was saying, 'I can't put up with all that noise in the classroom next to mine.'

'But Design and Technology is an important area of the curriculum, Felicity. The children have to do it somewhere now that this room's been condemned,' the Head replied.

The door to the woodstore opened a crack and the Head's face appeared, briefly silhouetted against the light. The children froze. Then the door closed smartly. They breathed again.

'. . . well, I don't see why they should have to do it next to my room . . . all that hammering and banging. It's not real work . . .' There was the rattle of a key and the click of a lock. The sound of the voices faded as the teachers walked away. And then the outside door slammed. The fugitives were alone, locked into the dark storeroom.

Sharon let out a great long sigh of despair, as though she'd been holding her breath all that time.

'He's locked us in. We're trapped.' She found the light switch and turned it on.

Diz tried the door. 'It's locked, all right. So – what are we going to do now?'

Sharon sat on a dusty wooden box and stared round the room.

'When we don't turn up for lessons they'll probably send out a search party.'

'But what if we're not missed?' asked Diz, gloomily. 'I've got English next and Old Nick never checks the register. We should have owned up.'

'Look,' said Sharon, feeling in her pockets for her last mint, 'this is the DT room, right?'

'So what?'

'Well, Design and Technology. Problem solving! We have to solve the problem of how to get out of here.'

'Ha, ha, ha. Very funny, I don't think. We could be here all night. They'll have the police out and everything.'

Sharon brushed some fluff from the mint and popped it into her mouth.

'I'm serious. There must be something in here we can use to break the door down or bust the lock. Look at all this stuff.'

The storeroom was certainly full of rubbish – it seemed like all the junk in the world had eventually found its way home. Although the room was small, it had a very high ceiling to accommodate the long planks of timber stored against the walls. As well as the wood – pine, mostly, with sheets of ply and hardboard – there were sheets of Perspex, large wooden boxes of half-finished projects, a damaged canoe slung across the ceiling, a huge model aeroplane without wings, an assortment of cans covered in dried-up goo, half a guitar, toppled columns of empty yoghurt cartons, a radio in pieces, a set of pram wheels, a broken washing machine, a stepladder to reach the high shelves and two large cupboards. Diz and Sharon began to examine these carefully.

'It's no good. They're both locked,' moaned Diz, giving one a hefty kick. 'Ouch! I've done my foot in now.' He sat down heavily on a crate of old-fashioned woodworking planes and nursed his toe.

Sharon gave each of the cupboard doors a last shake but she, too, had to admit defeat.

'I'm starving,' Diz complained. 'You could have shared your last sweet with me. We might not eat again for days. It's Friday, you know. Have you thought about that? We'll be in here all weekend.'

'Stop whinging. You're right; I should have given you the fluff. Look, there must be a way out of here. Let's give it a really good search. Maybe we'll find a hammer or a screwdriver that's fallen behind the shelves.'

'Or a secret door,' Diz said brightly, his mood changing. 'Perhaps a tunnel under the school. Maybe treasure.'

Sharon looked at Diz and sighed, as her mother often did. 'Oh yeah, sure.'

'Well, for your information, there is another door in this room and I can see it from here.' Diz folded his arms and looked pleased with himself. He knew his sister was smarter than he was — everybody said so — and it made him feel good to be one up on her.

Sharon stared around the room. What had she missed? In the end she had to give up. 'Well? Where is it, then? Is this a joke to get your own back?'

'Look. Up there!' Diz pointed at the ceiling. Sure enough, there was a trapdoor. 'If it leads up to the attic we may be able to get along to another classroom, one of the empty ones. Can you remember if any of the classroom ceilings have trap doors in them?'

Sharon couldn't. It was not the sort of thing she noticed — although she'd spent hours staring at the ceiling in French.

Together they hauled the stepladder across the floor and positioned it beneath the trapdoor. Diz put his foot hesitantly on the first rung. 'It's a long way up. I'm not sure about this. Hold it tightly now.' He was not very good at heights. Gingerly he began to climb the rickety ladder.

From the top he could easily reach the trapdoor. He pushed it as hard as he could, the ladder swaying dangerously all the while, but the wood held firm and he had to admit defeat. Discouraged, he climbed slowly back down.

Then Sharon had a bright idea. They manoeuvred one of the longest planks from its rack and, holding it tightly, held the heavy piece of wood beneath the trapdoor. On the count of three they thrust it upwards, knocking the trapdoor out of its frame with a resounding crack. The plank sprang from their grip and Diz just managed to dive out of its way as it divided a large sheet of Perspex into two. A cloud of dust enveloped them and Diz started coughing. 'As if we're not in enough trouble already,' he groaned.

'Come on,' Sharon said, already up the ladder. 'With a bit of luck we'll get out of all this and they'll never know it was us.' She disappeared from view.

Diz was half-way up when her face, by now looking rather grimy, peered down at him from the hole. 'It's dark up here. Have you got a torch?'

'Funnily enough I haven't got a torch on me today. I usually carry one to school. It comes in very handy when we have Environmental Studies in the attic.' He didn't hear her reply.

Soon Diz had joined his sister. It was dark, but

above them they could see thin streaks of pale daylight squeezing through the slates and, more importantly, a way through to what must be the loft of the main school building. To reach it they would have to climb over a brick wall about a metre and a half high, which formed a partition across the loft.

Diz leaned against the wall and searched his pockets for matches. He brought out two crumpled cigarettes.

'You're stupid, smoking,' Sharon said.

'Dad does.'

Sharon gave him her most withering look; she'd been saving it up. The effect was lost in the gloom.

Then something lying by the side of the trapdoor caught Diz's eye. 'Look! A box of matches.' He picked it up and rattled it. 'What a stroke of luck . . . Oh no!'

'What?'

'The matches are all dead. Oh, there's one live one. We'd better save that.' He slipped the matchbox into his pocket.

After further discussion – Diz was all for going back and yelling for help – they decided to lift an empty box from the storeroom up the ladder and use it to climb the wall. This proved easier than they had thought and they soon found themselves standing in the main school loft, only a little tired and breathless, before a blackness which stretched before them into infinity. Or so it seemed.

Suddenly both Diz and Sharon felt alone. Not only alone but also rather strange. If either had thought to explain it, they would have said it was like waking up in the night and not remembering where you were, or like travelling in a lift. Then there was a bump as though the lift had stopped. Tiny scraps of mortar and dust fell lightly around them.

'What was that?' Diz whispered.

'Maybe somebody slammed a door.'

Diz turned around and felt the wall they had climbed over.

'Sharon,' he whispered, 'how are we going to get back over it? We've left the box on the other side.'

Was it his imagination or did the wall seem higher than before? He ran his hands up the rough brick surface. Maybe this side of the attic was lower. A wall couldn't suddenly grow taller, could it?

'Don't worry,' Sharon was whispering back. 'We'll find a way out. We won't have to come back this way, will we?'

They crept forward, feeling their way carefully across the dusty ceiling joists of the old building.

'Do you know where we are?' Sharon whispered after a few minutes, her voice edged with uncertainty.

'In the school attic,' Diz replied. She fancied he was grinning, but in fact he was rather frightened and his face, were it visible, would have looked tight and serious.

'You know what I mean. Whereabouts over the school? I've lost my sense of direction. The French rooms are at the back of the DT room, aren't they? Seven and eight?'

'Yes, but I think we must be over room four now –'
Diz was cut short by Sharon's hand on his arm, making him jump.

'Listen,' she whispered, 'I can hear something.'

They stood very still in the darkness. 'There,' she said. 'Did you hear it?'

He strained his ears and then made it out too. A soft pitter-pattering sound. 'Mice?' he asked nervously.

'Or rats. I'm scared, Diz. Perhaps we should go back after all.' Sharon held his arm even more tightly. 'I know it sounds silly, but I feel like we're being watched.'

'Don't worry,' he said, trying to sound more courageous than he felt. 'It's only mice.' He gave his sister's hand a squeeze.

Still and quiet in the darkness, they caught another sound. A voice, in the distance ahead and below them. Cautiously, still feeling for the joists, they made their way towards the sound. Four lines of bright light cut a rectangle in the blackness beneath. A trapdoor.

Sharon put her lips very close to Diz's ear. 'Do you think you could open it very slightly without being heard?' He shook his head. It would be a foolish risk to take, having got this far, but he could see a tiny circle of light in the trapdoor big enough to peep through. At least he could find out their position. He slowly crouched down and brought his eye to the hole. Then gasped in amazement – and fear.

'What is it?' Sharon whispered urgently.

What Diz had seen was impossible. He must surely be dreaming. He looked up at his sister, his eyes wide with terror.

CHAPTER 2

THE BRETHREN

The classroom below looked normal enough. There were two large cupboards at the side. Grey curtains hung along the wall by the door. The bare walls were in need of a coat of paint and the desks were old and battered, although laid out neatly in rows. But there was something odd about the children.

They looked different. There were about a dozen sitting at the desks, leafing through reams of paper. Diz did not recognize any of them and they were not wearing school uniform but clothes that could best be described as rags. The children looked like their clothes, worn out and neglected.

Diz took in all this in an instant before his eyes turned to the thing that had so frightened him, standing at the front of the class. From a distance it might have passed for a man, but only just. It wore tight-fitting black clothes, mainly of leather, decorated with rusty iron studs and chains. Its skin was covered in black fur and its head was not human.

Diz stood up slowly, his face a pale white glow in the gloom. 'It's a dog, Sharon. A dog. I must be going mad.'

Impatiently Sharon crouched down in the dust and peered through the hole. Diz was right. She could hardly believe her eyes. The creature walking between the rows of children had the head of a dog. Large pointed ears poked through a black iron helmet and bloodshot eyes patrolled the class. It reminded Sharon of an Alsatian. Her uncle had had one once that had bitten her leg when she was climbing a wall. She didn't like them.

The creature was directly below her now. It stopped suddenly as if listening. She drew back. Could it smell them? She knew that Alsatians had a keenly developed sense of smell.

It walked on. Sharon was shaking.

'What are we going to do?' she whispered very, very softly.

'I don't know. Listen.'

The dog creature was talking. 'Have you all finished?' A pause. 'Take your paper to the chute. Make haste. If you are late there will be no supper.' His voice was not as loud as they might have expected. Rather, it was quiet and cold. There was a nasty, menacing edge to it that made them both shiver.

They heard the class leave. Diz sat down on a joist. 'I just don't know what to say. Is it a joke?'

'I don't think so. It's creepy, isn't it?'

'Creepy's not the word. I'm scared stiff.' Diz bent down to the hole again. 'I can hear somebody crying.'

The class and the dog creature had gone, but sitting on his own at the back, his head on his arms, was a boy. He was sobbing softly to himself.

'Look, someone's still there,' Diz whispered. 'What shall we do?'

'Let's go back to the storeroom.'

'Don't you think we should help him?'

'Well, I'm not going down there. Are you?'

'I see what you mean.' Diz said. They sat in silence for a couple of minutes, trying to make sense of what they'd seen. 'Well,' Diz continued, 'if we could shift this trapdoor that boy might be able to tell us what's going on. We don't have to go down there.'

Reluctantly Sharon agreed. Diz grabbed the handle, bracing himself with his knees bent and feet against the joists.

'I'm not sure this is a very good idea,' Sharon murmured.

Diz pulled.

The trapdoor lifted easily. Diz, who had been expecting the door to be heavy, and stuck, stumbled, almost fell, and dropped the door with a clatter on the joists. The noise seemed deafening. Hesitantly, Diz peered through the hole. The boy was staring up, wide-eyed with alarm.

Diz gave what he hoped was a smile. 'Don't be scared.' The pot calling the kettle black, he thought. 'What's your name?'

The boy stared up at him as though he'd seen a ghost.

'Jaro,' he mumbled.

'Hello, Jaro,' Diz said brightly.

Jaro looked about Diz's age but he was a little smaller. He had long, blond, unkempt hair and blue eyes. He was as scruffy as the other children – but there was more vitality about him, despite his tears.

There was a pause as the two boys stared at one another, neither knowing what to say. Sharon squeezed her head into the gap. 'What are you doing here?' she asked.

'What are *you*?' Jaro asked back.

'This is getting us nowhere,' Diz said to Sharon. 'I'm going down.'

'No! Stay here with me.'

'I'll be all right.'

Sharon drew back to give her brother room. 'Are you sure?'

'Don't worry,' Diz said bravely, more bravely than he felt. He gripped the trapdoor frame firmly, swung down and, in a cloud of dust, landed lightly and safely on a desk.

'Atishoo!' The dust made him sneeze and the sneeze sounded as loud as a bomb going off. Diz glanced round nervously and pulled a tissue out of his pocket. The matchbox fell out and clattered on to the desk by his feet. At that moment there was a noise outside the room and the mumble of voices. Diz was across the room in a second, crouching behind one of the cupboards as the door opened. The dog creature had returned.

Jaro glanced anxiously at Diz. If the creature came right in it would spot him easily. Jaro stood and walked forward, picking up the tell-tale box as inconspicuously as possible, hoping his quick action wouldn't be noticed. It wasn't. The creature laughed a mean laugh. 'Eager for your punishment eh, whelp?' He grabbed Jaro by the neck and marched him out the room. The door slammed.

Diz was sweating. He looked up and realized the open trapdoor was in full view and dust still hung in the air. It was a wonder he hadn't been caught. They had been lucky. Sharon's white face peered down. 'Are you all right?'

'No, I'm half left.'

'Very funny.'

'I'm coming back up. Quick!'

But even by standing on the desk and jumping, with Sharon's arms waving to catch him, Diz could not reach the trapdoor. He hunted frantically around the room for something else to stand on, but there was nothing. Not even a waste-paper bin to upturn. He tried the cupboards, but they were locked.

'Perhaps I should come down there,' Sharon called softly.

'No. We'll both be stuck then.'

'Shall I have a hunt up here? I might find some rope or something.'

'That's a good idea,' Diz said, 'and maybe I could pile up the desks.'

Sharon disappeared. To Diz's dismay, he found the desks were bolted to the floor. Then something struck him as odd. It was so obvious he was surprised he hadn't noticed it before. The room had no outside windows.

Anyone who's ever been out on a dark night with the wind whistling through the trees and thought there was somebody following them, will know how Sharon felt as she gingerly made her way across the joists. She thought she heard footsteps. But when she stopped,

17

they stopped. Surely only echoes, she told herself, bits of old plaster she must have dislodged.

She fancied she saw red pin-pricks of light, like tiny eyes. But no; she must be imagining it. Then she heard the pattering noises again. By now she was some distance from the light of the trapdoor and it was getting difficult to see. There didn't seem to be any rope lying around. It had been a stupid idea after all, and she decided to go back. Again the rat noises.

Then the trapdoor banged back into place and the attic was plunged into darkness. Sharon shrieked.

'Don't be afraid,' a voice said. 'We won't hurt you.'

A weak torch beam lit the attic. Six creatures, each half Sharon's size, stood in a shadowy circle around her.

Sharon was close to panic – how could she cope with this? But she stood her ground and tried to be calm. After all, nothing could be worse than the dog they'd seen, and these creatures seemed friendly. Each was covered in soft brown fur, wore a coarse, brown robe, had a long tail and bright, intelligent eyes. She was surrounded by giant mice.

She thought that they would have made a funny cartoon. But the world of sitting at home with her mum watching cartoons on the television seemed a long way away. Sharon suddenly felt tearful.

One of the mice stepped forward. He was slightly larger than the others. Then he spoke. 'It's all right,' he said. 'We'll look after you. We give rest to weary Children. My name's Reginald.' He gave a little bow. 'May I introduce Bartholomew, Gladly, Doughty,

Jeroboam and Nigel.' Each mouse bowed solemnly in turn.

'It is foretold,' Reginald went on, 'that travellers will come. Strangers to this place. And their coming will be as the rain to the desert or the sun to the dawn.'

'Shush!' said the mouse called Bartholomew. 'You don't go telling that sort of information to just anybody, oh no. Deary me, she could be a spy.'

'Ooh, yes, a spy, a spy. Deary me,' the other mice chipped in.

Sharon felt bewildered. 'But who are you? What's going on?'

'Poor child,' Reginald said. 'We are the Brethren. We live and work here in the roof of the world, helping the Children until such time as the prophecy is –'

'There you go again,' interrupted Bartholomew, 'telling her things. We know nothing about her. I mean, she's obviously not one of the Children, is she?'

Nigel stepped forward. 'Who are you, child?'

'My name is Sharon Gillespie. I really don't know what's going on. I came here with my brother. We were trying to find a way to escape from the woodstore.'

A murmur went around the mice. 'The woodstore, eh? Oh, so the woodstore, is it?'

'Er . . . what's the woodstore?' Nigel asked.

'Well –' Sharon was about to explain when she suddenly realized what a weird situation she was in. 'Er . . . look,' she said, 'mice don't talk where we come from.'

More murmuring among the mice. 'Mice don't talk? Deary me, whatever next.'

'Please tell me where we are and how we can get home.'

Reginald blew his nose on a red hanky he had pulled out from under his robe. He addressed his companions. 'I think we should escort her to the palace. She seems truthful enough to me. What do you say, Barth?'

Bartholomew sniffed. 'Well, I suppose there can't be any harm in it. She doesn't look like Howen, anyway. But I still think she might be a spy.'

'It's a decision for the Abbot,' piped up Gladly.

One of the mice giggled.

'What are Howen?' Sharon asked.

'The dogs are the Howen. A mean and vicious breed they are, too,' Bartholomew said.

Reginald lightly touched Sharon's arm and fixed her with his bright eyes. 'Will you come with us?' he asked.

'But what about Diz? He went down to that class-room and he can't get back up.'

'Your brother . . . the boy? No problem. Nigel!' Reginald said. 'You know what to do. And hurry.'

Nigel scampered lightly over the joists into the darkness and reappeared seconds later with a rope ladder.

'Let's go!' Reginald commanded and together they made their way to the trapdoor. Nigel peered into the hole. 'All clear.' He lifted the trapdoor and Sharon looked down into the room.

It was empty.

CHAPTER 3

THE REBELS

Alice, a small, pale-faced twelve year old, was standing next to her master in the hall, her eyes downcast. 'Sit!' the creature named Bull barked. Meekly she sat. The Howen gave the girl a casual kick with his iron-toed boot and turned his attention back to the stage.

Raffer, the leader's lieutenant, paced nervously, waiting for the master to appear. Wiry white curls tumbled around his uniform of creased, black leather. A rapier dangled loosely from his waist, its handle studded with black jewels, its scabbard of silk and leather. He was toying anxiously with a long, thin ceremonial bone, carved with strange symbols.

The hall was typical of a gym at any small old-fashioned school in all but one respect. There were no windows to the outside world. The only light came from a row of electric lights set behind small circles of opaque glass in the high, curved ceiling. There were wall bars. The floor was of wood parquet, although its shine had long been worn away, and slung across the back of the stage hung a flag. It had a black

21

background with a white circle, cut by a red streak of lightning.

Twenty-three Howen were gathered in the hall and of these, five had children cowering at their feet on leather leads. The room stank of dog.

The shuffling of armour, the grunts and whines suddenly stopped and a thick silence hung in the air. Even the thousands of tiny hairs, which made dust clouds in the air, stopped swirling around and hung suspended in the atmosphere. The leader was making his entrance.

In the human world he would have been called a Great Dane. Here he was a monster, half as tall again as any of the other Howen. His name was Feer. He was covered in armour of dull metal, festooned with thousands of tiny white pearls, many of which had fallen off, leaving patches of worn leather showing through. A huge sword hung from his waist. Alice could feel the thud of his heavy boots along the wooden floor as he walked slowly towards the stage. From beneath an iron helmet, emblazoned with the lightning symbol, peered large, blood-red eyes. His teeth were yellow and fang-like. He wore no collar but from his neck hung a large triangular prism of blue crystal that seemed to glow with its own light. Saliva dribbled copiously from his jowls on to the stage.

The silence grew as Feer held his followers in his spell. Then he threw back his head and began to growl. Slowly the low, rumbling moan grew, becoming louder, higher. Another Howen took up the call. And another. And another. The howl grew louder. Now every creature had its head arched, jaws stretched, baying. The howl became a deafening roar. The human pets put their hands over their ears to keep out the dreadful noise. The room seemed to vibrate, to shake. Then, as if by some unseen signal, it stopped. Silence rushed into the void.

In a voice as soft as cotton wool, but full of menace, Feer spoke.

'There is a scent. It is the scent of a child, but it is not one of the Children. There is an interloper in our midst and it must be sniffed out.'

The Howen shuffled and looked around nervously. An interloper, thought Bull. What does that mean?

'There is nothing to be scared of,' said Feer, as though picking up the Howen's unspoken thoughts. 'It is just the scent of a child. Blood discovered it.'

A murmur of approval ran round the hall.

'We must find this child and find out what it means to us. Raffer!' The lieutenant looked up. 'Gather the Children here and then search the building. The scent is strange and strong. We will easily find it.'

Raffer nodded excitedly.

Feer stood a moment longer, gazing over the pack. The hall became deathly still. 'So,' the huge dog snarled. 'What are we waiting for? Let us begin.' He turned and marched from the room.

There was pandemonium as the Howen all began talking at once. Raffer, waving his ceremonial bone in the air, was trying to make his thin voice heard above the din.

Bull yanked his pet to her feet. 'Come, girl,' he said. 'This could be fun.'

*

23

Sharon picked her way with difficulty over the joists in the attic, guided only by the weak torch beam. She felt both angry and desperately sad. Diz had been captured by those horrible things and now she was being taken to meet the Abbot with a bunch of mice called the Brethren. It was like a dream, but she knew she wasn't going to wake up. It was crazy.

She wished she had been nicer to her brother. She loved him, but he got on her nerves so, rushing into things before thinking them through. She would be much nicer to him in the future, if she ever saw him again. She could feel the tears welling up.

They had searched the classroom and Nigel had even ventured out into the corridor, but to no avail. Nothing. No Diz. It's a good job it's dark, Sharon thought. I can't let these mice see I'm scared and miserable.

They had been walking for some time when they heard the eerie sound.

'What's that?' Sharon said, startled.

Now she realized it was a strange wail, growing louder all the time. She shivered. 'It gives me the creeps.'

'It's all right,' said Nigel, putting his paw on her shoulder. 'It's a Howen meet. They make that noise when they get together. You'll get used to it.'

The thought of more dogs like the one she'd seen, enough to make all that noise, made Sharon shudder.

The noise stopped as abruptly as it had started.

'Do they often get together?' Sharon asked.

'Usually only on important occasions,' Reginald said from the front. Maybe they've found your brother, he thought. But he didn't mention this to Sharon.

Soon the going became harder. The floor joists were closer together, but they were warped. There were also more roof supports and beams and Sharon found herself continually having to duck and dodge. The mice made their way through the maze with ease.

'We live along the Edge,' Reginald said. 'The Howen rarely come this way and we can make foraging expeditions fairly safely.'

'What do you eat?'

'There's only greyroot and greyfruit. Nothing else grows in the building.'

'What do the Howen eat?'

'Mice. If they get the chance,' said Bartholomew from the back.

'They eat greyroot, too. But meat as well, if they can find it,' said Nigel. 'Mainly insects; the place is crawling with them. They don't like it, but it's all there is. They even eat the spiders – if they can catch them. Disgraceful.'

An image of the dogs eating human flesh came into Sharon's mind. She quickly expelled it and shuddered. She didn't mind insects or spiders but better not tell Diz about them. He didn't like insects, and spiders terrified him, although he'd never let on. If he was all right . . .

She laspsed into silence again.

At last they reached their destination. The Brethren melted into the darkness, leaving Sharon with Nigel.

'Wait here,' he said. 'The Abbot will be along to see you in a moment.' Then he too stepped into the darkness and was gone.

She was standing outside a room built into the attic.

She stepped in. The walls, floor and ceiling were of bare wood, slightly bowed, which gave the room a strange shape.

Nigel came in through the opposite door. 'His Serene Highness, the Abbot,' he announced grandly.

The Abbot entered. 'Welcome to our palace, oh stranger,' he said.

Sharon stared at him incredulously. Then she smiled. Then she laughed out loud.

'Wait!' Moke peered round the corner. 'All clear!'

The three boys ran as quietly as they could down the corridor, ducking low as they passed the classroom windows. Diz was in the middle and Crab brought up the rear.

Waiting for Sharon in that strange classroom had seemed to go on for ever and so Diz had decided to find out what was outside the room. There he had met the two boys who had told him he was in danger, and insisted he follow them.

'Where are we going?' whispered Diz.

'Shhh,' Moke hissed over his shoulder. 'Don't talk – run. If we're caught we're done for.'

Moke and Crab were dressed like the other children Diz had seen. Moke was about Diz's age, thin, dark-skinned, with long black hair. Crab was much younger and smaller, also very thin, with straggly, brown hair and a pale complexion.

After only a few minutes of running down the dusty corridors, they reached a dead end – a cloak-room. It was partly panelled in stained green wood and there were two rows of empty coat hooks, a couple of mildewed urinals and a row of sinks against the far wall. Diz tried one of the taps. A thin trickle of brown water gurgled out.

Moke went to the furthest sink and yanked at the basin. It swung easily away from the wall, supported by its plumbing, to reveal a large hole. Moke removed some loose bricks and climbed through. The other two followed. As they crawled into the darkness Diz heard Crab slide everything back into place. It was suddenly pitch black. 'Bend down,' ordered Moke, as he moved off into the darkness. Diz followed. They were going quite fast and Diz had to feel his way. Twice he banged his head and he caught his trousers on something sharp and cut his knee.

'We only found this tunnel a few weeks ago. It leads to some deserted rooms. That's where our hide-out is. The Howen haven't found it yet.'

'They've been close a few times,' said Crab.

'Too many scents, too confusing. They're not as sharp as they were. I think they're losing their sense of smell.'

'Who are the Howen?' asked Diz.

'The dogs, of course.'

Diz pinched himself for the seventh time. He didn't wake up. He still wasn't dreaming. What was it all about? Where was Sharon? Was she OK? Perhaps she'd found her way back to their school. Maybe he was here all alone.

'Ouch!' Moke had stopped and Diz had bumped into him.

'You can stand up,' whispered Crab. Diz felt above his head: nothing but air. He stood slowly, just in case. His knee was beginning to throb. He heard a click and then a door opened and they were stepping out of a cupboard into a dimly lit corridor.

It was narrow – barely room for the boys to walk in single file – and the floor was covered in loose and broken wooden tiles. The ceiling was very high. The shape of the whole place was wrong, thought Diz, kind of elongated.

'The Howen find these pathways difficult,' Moke said. 'They get narrower as you get nearer to the Edge. We don't go there much, though. Gives us the creeps.'

'The Edge?' Diz queried.

'Yes, further away from the main rooms. Everywhere gets kind of squashed up.'

'Is this building really a school?' Diz asked.

'What's a school?'

The question took Diz by surprise. After all, they were in one. Perhaps the boy was joking. 'It doesn't matter,' he replied.

They came to a doorway. The door that had filled it was lying across the floor. Carefully Diz followed his new companions across the threshold. They were in a long, narrow room. It was impossible to say what colour it had once been. Now it was grey. The light from a tiny disc in the ceiling flickered every few seconds, as though it couldn't bear to see such a depressing scene.

Sitting on grubby cushions and blankets along one wall were six children, three boys and three girls. Their clothes were ragged, dirty and torn and their faces as grey as the walls. But their eyes were alive. They jumped to their feet and gathered excitedly round the stranger, staring at him in amazement, while Moke and Crab stood to one side.

One of the girls reached forward and rubbed the sleeve of Diz's jacket between her fingers, as though she'd never seen such a thing before.

'Who are you?' she asked.

'Richard Gillespie. My friends call me Diz.'

'We found him wandering around the corridors,' said Moke. 'He was lucky.'

'I'm Els.' At first glance the girl reminded Diz of Sharon. She was taller and bigger built, but her eyes and mouth were very much like his sister's. She immediately gave the impression of being a leader, someone used to having her own way.

'Where have you come from?' Els asked. 'We haven't seen you before.'

'Well . . .' How could he explain such a weird thing? 'I'm from . . . er . . . Earth, I suppose. Is this Earth? I was at school with Sharon, that's my sister . . . and we got trapped in the DT room –'

'Hang on,' Els said. 'I don't understand any of that. Earth? School? DT room?'

Diz explained again, answering as many questions as he could, until they seemed reasonably satisfied. He knew so little himself that it was hard work.

'Look,' he finished, 'I really don't know anything about this place. Who are *you*? Who are the dog people . . . the Howen? What is this place?'

'We're not really sure,' Moke said, 'but we think it's a prison of some kind. We were taken from our homes years ago. None of us remember much about how we got here.'

'I remember there was a big fight, a battle of some kind,' Els said. 'There was a lot of noise and confusion. I think we were brought here until it was safe again.'

'But it never was safe,' Moke went on. 'No one came for us, did they? And we found there was no way out, we were trapped. Then the Howen arrived and had us sorting out the paper.'

'Tons and tons of the stuff,' said Els. 'But we escaped from the Howen. Nine of us. One at a time. The mice helped us, of course. We're the Rebels. Are you going to join us? Do you know the way out?'

Diz thought back to the wall in the attic that they had climbed over. He remembered the strange feeling he'd had when he felt the wall, how it had suddenly seemed much higher. Was it now blocking their way back? That was silly, impossible; walls didn't suddenly grow. But deep down he knew. He, too, was trapped in this awful place. Then something else the girl had said registered.

'Mice? Did you say mice helped you?' Diz wondered if he'd heard right. But then nothing ought to surprise him now.

'Yes, the mice. The Brethren. They live in the attic.'

Diz thought of Sharon. 'My sister's in the attic,' he said.

'She'll be safe then,' Els replied. 'The mice are all right.'

Moke was looking around anxiously.

'Where's Baloney?'

'Doing lookout.'

'We didn't see him. We should have passed him.'

They all looked at one another in alarm.

'What's that?' whispered Els.

They listened. There was no doubt about it. Along the corridor could be heard a shuffling sound and the rattle of loose floor tiles.

'Howen!'

CHAPTER 4

THE PROWLER

Jaro stood next to his friend Bel. At least she would laugh at the jokes he made now and again. She still had some spirit left, not like most of the other Children. They were all standing in the hall in rows. It was the end of the day and they were tired. Most of the Howen were taking part in the hunt; there were only two in the hall. One stood at the front and the other lounged against the wall bars, scratching himself and gazing vacantly into space.

Jaro often wondered why the Children simply didn't overpower the Howen – they outnumbered them by so many. But then, looking at the rows of dejected, pale faces staring into the weary silence, he knew why. He would have to join the Rebels soon, before he, too, became like the others. But did he have the nerve? That was his constant problem.

Bel whispered to Jaro, 'What's it all about?' She was as tall as Jaro but a year younger. Her long black hair was tied in a pony tail by a ribbon that had once been pink. If freed, her hair would reach her waist. She was intelligent and kind and, like Jaro, one of the

few Children who had managed to keep her wits abou·
her. They would escape to the Rebels together, Jaro
thought.

She whispered again. 'What's it all about? We should
be in bed by now.'

Jaro thought the fuss must be to do with the boy
from the attic. Should he tell Bel? She wouldn't tell
the Howen, of course, but she might tell one of her
friends . . . and if a rumour started and the Howen
picked it up. . . . He shuddered.

'Dunno,' he whispered back.

'I've never seen them so excited. If we're not sent to
bed soon I'll be asleep standing up.'

'You two!' a voice barked. The Howen by the wall
bars had stopped scratching and had noticed them.
'Stop talking or you'll do double time in the latrines tomorrow.'

They fell silent, staring at the floor. Secretly Jaro
slid his hand in his pocket and felt the strange, small
wooden box that the boy from the attic had dropped.
The boy they were hunting right now. He hoped they
wouldn't catch him.

The Brethren were crowded around Sharon in the
palace and, like Sharon, they too were laughing. The
Abbot was standing as straight as he could, trying to
look important. On his head was a tall hat made of
cardboard rolled to a point.

'Why do you laugh?' the Abbot asked Sharon. 'Do
you laugh at *your* abbot?'

'We don't have an abbot, exactly,' Sharon said. 'We
do have monasteries and abbeys so I suppose we have

'. . . well . . . I suppose I just wasn't expect-
. . . it was that funny hat I think. I'm sorry I
. . . ed.'

'I see.'

'And relief. I was scared earlier. Seeing you in that
hat . . . well . . .'

'Quite,' the Abbot muttered. He reached up and
adjusted the hat, which had slid to an odd angle.

'After all, they say a cat can look at a queen. Why
not an abbot?' Sharon gave the giant mouse a friendly
smile.

'We'll have no more cat talk, if you please.' The
Abbot shivered and smoothed his whiskers with his
paw.

'And I didn't realize it was going to be you, Reginald, either.'

'Well, I don't make a big thing about being abbot,'
Reginald said, examining his paws. 'When we fulfil
our destiny it will be different.' Trying to be as casual
as he could, he took his hat off and gave it to Nigel.

'What do you mean, "fulfil our destiny"?' asked
Sharon.

Reginald looked thoughtful. 'As we grow, we
change. And our growing and changing is somehow
linked to our leaving, the time when we must leave
this place. That is our destiny, although *how* we will
escape is unclear. I must say, the thought of growing
up is a bit frightening.'

'I see,' Sharon said, although she didn't see at all.

'Haven't you ever wondered what it will be like –
growing up? No matter. Bartholomew's right. I
shouldn't be telling you such things. Not yet, anyway.

34

For the time being we are the Brethren. We have to do what we can for the Children. They are such poor things now. So different from when they arrived.'

'How were they then?' Sharon asked.

'Happy,' Reginald said. 'Innocent, a little frightened, perhaps. Some of them were only just walking. There was laughter then, of course. We played with them and found them food. There was plenty of it in those days. Then the Howen arrived; that's when we moved up here. The Howen were hungry. They thought we were food.' Reginald and the mice were suddenly very quiet. Sharon broke the silence.

'How did *you* get here, then?'

'We were crossing the Moon Mountains on a quest.'

'Well, it was more of a game, really.' Nigel added.

'Sort of a test,' Barth said, 'although we shouldn't really be telling you this in case you're a spy.'

'Anyway,' Reginald went on, 'we came across an old tumbledown building. There was a storm coming and it seemed like a good place to shelter. But once we were inside it we found we couldn't get out. We were trapped.'

'We've been here ever since,' Nigel sighed.

'Would you like a guided tour?' Reginald asked. Sharon nodded and smiled.

'Then follow me.'

Sharon would never have said – not wanting to risk offending the mice again – but as palaces went it was rather disappointing. Nothing like Buckingham Palace or the palaces she'd seen on television. There were six rooms altogether. Each room was buckled and out of shape. Each was dimly lit. The light came up through gaps in the floorboards – laid unevenly over the crooked joists – from small, empty rooms below that the Howen were too big to use. Three of the attic rooms were living space, full of blankets and straw, one was empty and one was a store, piled with something that Reginald said was dried greyroot and greyfruit.

They came to the sixth room. 'What's that?' Sharon asked. 'Is it a game of some kind?'

A wooden board lay on the floor. A large circle had been painted on it in dark brown. A smaller circle had been drawn inside it and a smaller circle inside that. Sharon counted seven circles altogether, each getting smaller. Then four lines from edge to edge, each crossing through the centre, divided the circles into eight equal sections.

Pieces of elegantly carved wood stood in various sections of the circle.

'Yes, it is a game. But it's also very serious,' Reginald said.

'It looks a bit like chess,' Sharon ventured.

'It's called the Game of Changes,' Reginald went on. 'The game has been with the Brethren since time began; that's what the legends say. Really it's a puzzle and its completion brings a time of change.'

'Is that your destiny, then?' Sharon asked.

'In a way. Some pieces represent us – the Brethren. Others represent things that have happened or might happen. The aim of the puzzle is to move the Brethren pieces to the centre in the correct way. Then the events shown on the board will come true.'

'I'm not sure I understand.'

'No matter,' Reginald said.

'Do you play it for fun, then?'

Reginald looked very serious for a moment, then relaxed and laughed. 'Of course.'

They moved on. The rooms were connected in a kind of circle and they found themselves back where they'd started.

'There are only six of you, then.' Sharon had thought there must be more. 'You can't do much for the Children, can you?'

'Not a lot. But we do what we can. We help the Rebels – the Children who have run away from the Howen. They're fed up with hiding. They want to overcome the Howen and escape.'

'How can they do that?'

'That's the tricky part. For one thing the Rebels are few and the Children are a pathetic lot. It's not their fault, though, poor things. They've been here a long time and most of them have lost the will to survive. And they're not in the best of health: a diet of greyroot and greyfruit isn't really enough. They don't eat insects. Not like the Howen, of course.'

'Ugh!' Sharon pulled a face.

'Neither do we. Especially not the spiders. We believe that the spiders are somehow woven into the Game. But they keep their own counsel and we have little to do with them.

'There's also the question of escape,' Reginald went on. 'Nobody has found a way out yet. Not even the Howen. That's why they spend so much time sifting through the paper. They think it holds the answer.

The Big Cheese spews it out and the Howen make the Children sort through it. But there's not much point really. No one knows what they're looking for.'

'What's this Big Cheese, then?'

'It's a machine of some kind. The Howen worship it. They think it's a god. Really, they're not all that bright. We call it the Big Cheese for a joke but even so, we keep out of its way. It is very powerful . . . and evil.'

A machine that spills out paper, thought Sharon. Could it be . . . Diz would know. But where was he? Was he safe? He might not have been captured by the Howen after all. He might even be with the Rebels. She hoped so. But if not, at least the Rebels might know where he was. She wondered what the time was. They would be missed at school by now.

There was something else worrying her: she needed the toilet. What did the Brethren do about that? She plucked up courage and asked Reginald.

'Well . . .' The Abbot frowned thoughtfully. 'There are some down below that the Children use. We usually go out near the Edge, this place is so vast. Look, I'll show you the way. Then we'll try and find the Rebels. They might know where your brother is. Or maybe we'll visit the Big Cheese first. Would that be a good idea?'

'Can you take me back to where you found me?' Sharon asked. 'Perhaps we can get out the same way we came in.'

'We can try,' Reginald said, 'but I wouldn't hold out too much hope.'

*

The great beast was known as the Prowler. It moaned softly to itself as it dragged its massive body through the underground rooms and cellars of the building's lowest level. The cellars were damp and dark and the beast was hunting for food. Its body was tired and weary, broken, but its senses were, as always, fully alert. It followed the same pathway, over cold stone, through open doorways, past artefacts from an alien world, questing about for subtle temperature changes. A source of heat might mean sustenance. Listening, too, for tell-tale noises: for footsteps, the murmur of voices, the brush of clothing against a bare brick wall. Alert for unusual scents: the smell of dog, or mouse, or child.

It arched an arm and dragged a claw-like feeler along the ceiling, dislodging rotten plaster and dust. Nothing there. It had no sense of present time but knew that its own time was running out. It must find food soon or it would die. It passed a vine of greyroot, probably dropped by a Howen. Greyroot would not satisfy its craving. It was hungry for a very different kind of food.

The Rebels looked at one another in dismay. The noises in the corridor outside their hideout were getting louder. Were the Howen so close? Els's urgent whisper broke the silence.

'Run! We'll meet at Far Point.'

Too late. The noise was outside the doorway now. Diz held his breath.

A large boy appeared, red-faced and breathless. He clattered over the fallen door and sat heavily on a cushion. Diz breathed a sigh of relief.

'What's up, Baloney?' Els asked quickly.

Baloney reminded Diz of a fat boy he knew who had lost a lot of weight. He wondered what they all ate. Come to think of it, he was hungry himself. A quarter pounder would go down a treat right now.

'Howen,' Baloney said, getting his breath back, 'and they're everywhere. I think they're searching for us.'

'It's him,' a voice said. All eyes turned to the tall, thin, pale-faced boy who had spoken. He had a shock of ginger hair hanging dirty and lank over his shoulders. 'They're after him, of course.' He pointed accusingly at Diz. 'He's responsible. If we give him up they'll leave us alone.'

'Ginger!' Moke said, surprised. 'You can't give someone up to the Howen.'

'He's not one of us,' the boy replied. 'He'll only give us away.'

One or two of the group muttered in agreement.

'No,' Els said firmly. 'The Howen are evil. If we hand Diz over ... well, that will make us as bad as them. We must do everything we can to be rid of them and I think Diz can help.'

'I say he goes,' Ginger said.

'Me too,' another voice agreed.

Diz was feeling very uncomfortable by now. He'd only just met these people. They'd saved him from the awful dog creatures and now they were discussing whether to hand him over to them, like a bag of bones from the butcher's. A wave of loneliness washed over him. Where was he? A long way from home. How far? A mile? A million miles? He wanted to be home with his mum, watching television, or out with his dad, walking the dog. Well – maybe not walking the dog. He wasn't sure how he'd feel about dogs when he got back. *If* he got back. Or even arguing with his sister. Sharon! Where was she? I'm sorry, Sharon, he thought, I won't make fun of you any more. Where are you?

'Look!' said Els angrily, 'I'm the leader and I say he stays. Come on. It's no use bickering. The Howen could be here any moment.'

Ginger stood before her and made a fist. 'Oh yeah? Well, I say we give him up.'

This is terrible, Diz thought. He pushed through the group and ran to the doorway. He felt hurt.

'Ginger's right,' he said. 'It's me they want. I'll lead them away.' He turned and ran.

'Wait for me,' Moke yelled and ran after him.

Diz slowed down and Moke caught him up.

'Ginger isn't so bad,' Moke said. 'He only wants to protect us. If we're caught the Children will have no chance. Look, you're right. We'll lead the Howen away. I know all the secret ways.' He gave Diz a friendly squeeze on the arm. 'We'll lead them a merry dance. OK?'

Diz smiled. He felt a little better. 'OK.'

But the smile was short-lived. The Howen were around the next corner.

CHAPTER 5

CAPTURED

It was Sharon's turn to go down the rope ladder to the empty classroom. She and the mice were going to look for Diz – and to visit the Big Cheese. They must have spent an hour searching in the attic for the low wall that she and Diz had climbed over. But it had gone. Sharon had felt close to despair then, knowing that she and Diz were trapped in this place too.

Bartholomew stayed at the top while Nigel held the ladder steady at the bottom. Sharon climbed down the narrow rungs carefully; they had not really been designed for a human. She was very aware that she was heading into danger. Real danger. Not just a telling-off by somebody stupid like the Witch but a terrible and personal danger, like arguing with somebody who held a *real* gun.

They crept from the classroom into the corridor outside. Gladly reappeared from scouting ahead and gave them the paws-up sign, and then she, Nigel, Reginald and Gladly made their way forward. Jeroboam, Bartholomew and Doughty were not coming with them. They had other things to do.

'We must be very quiet,' Reginald whispered. 'Especially near the dormitories. Normally the Children would be asleep by now, and most of the Howen too, but there's a lot of activity tonight.' He pulled out the big red hanky and blew his nose.

'Shh,' Nigel whispered.

'Don't shh me, I'm the Abbot,' Reginald retorted.

'Shh,' whispered Gladly from the front.

'Don't the Howen know about this trapdoor?' Sharon asked quietly.

'Of course they do. But we have several and they can't guard them all. They've been into the attic a couple of times but it's cramped up there and they have trouble walking over the joists. So in the main they leave us alone. They don't seem to think we're much of a threat.'

'Why don't the Rebels hide in the attic, then?'

'Well, for one thing, it's very dark up there and for another, with the Rebels there it would no longer be safe for anyone. The Howen would make a determined effort to root us all out.'

They had been walking for some time now with Gladly a little ahead to warn them of approaching danger. Sharon wondered what would happen if they met any Howen. She shuddered at the thought. She had only had the one brief glimpse of a Howen but, if anything, that image had grown more frightening in her mind.

'How big is this place?' Sharon asked.

'Pretty big. We haven't ever measured it,' said Nigel.

A lot bigger than our school, Sharon thought.

Some of the rooms they passed had windows that looked out on to the corridor but all were curtained and Sharon couldn't see in. The unmistakable smell of dog was everywhere. But this was no ordinary dog smell. The Howen smell was worse. There was something unhealthy about it – evil, Sharon thought.

They turned into a large, concreted area, which looked like an old-fashioned kitchen. Along one wall there were great, black iron cookers, with blue enamel oven doors and greasy white handles. Chipped and cracked white tiles lined the walls. There were huge vats, taller than Sharon, and squat wooden tables like enormous flat-backed insects, crouching, waiting.

But something was missing, Sharon noticed: food. There was no food of any kind, nor any waste. The kitchen was derelict.

'We must be very quiet now,' Reginald whispered as they left the kitchen. 'We are very close to the Howen.'

As quiet as a mouse, thought Sharon and grinned half-heartedly to herself.

They were silently making their way along a curving corridor when a flight of steps leading down appeared ahead of them. At that same moment Gladly materialized, puffing and panting.

'Howen!'

'Quick! In here!' Reginald opened a door and they scrambled into one of the classrooms. No sooner had the door closed than the corridor was full of noise.

'Where now?' a boy's voice yelled.

'This way!' a second voice commanded.

Running feet were followed by the sound of Howen

giving chase; yelps, yowls, the clatter of heavy boots. It all took seconds.

Sharon felt her heart beating wildly. Her mouth was dry.

'What's wrong?' Nigel asked. 'You look as though you've seen a ghost. You're white.'

Sharon just stood there, feeling the room swaying around her. At last she spoke. 'That was Diz, my brother. He just ran by. That was his voice . . . he . . . chased by those dogs . . .'

'Listen!'

Faraway somebody was yelling and swearing. Then the cries stopped.

'Oh no,' Sharon whispered, 'they've caught him.'

Nigel put his arm around her waist. 'Don't worry, child. He'll be all right, I'm sure.' She shrugged him off.

'If they hurt him I'll kill them,' she hissed, clenching and unclenching her fists.

'Come,' Reginald said quietly. 'There's nothing we can do right now. We must hurry ourselves or we might be caught, too. It's dangerous to stay around here for too long.'

Gladly peered around the door and beckoned them on; he was going to stay behind and await their return. They quickly crossed the corridor to the top of the staircase and made their way down the spiral steps into darkness. Sharon's anger began to fade as fear of the unknown took the upper hand. At the bottom, Reginald switched on his torch. 'This is the lower level,' he whispered.

Shadows leapt around them, cast by the great white

pillars that must support the building. Through the archways between the pillars was a blackness too deep for the torch beam to penetrate. And all around the damp corridors was a cold, unfriendly, empty darkness. Dark shapes danced around them like phantom tigers stalking an invisible prey.

Sharon shrank closer to Nigel as they made their way slowly forward. No, she suddenly thought, why should she be scared? She was Sharon Gillespie. They weren't going to make her feel small. She was taller than the mice, anyway. And who were *they*? The *they* that people always talked about? She'd survived her parents' separation. She'd jolly well survive this. She stepped boldly forward, her eyes bright with determination in the half light.

There was a noise. Not a human noise, but one that seemed to belong to the underground. A dark, secret thing.

'What's that?' Sharon whispered.

'The Prowler. It's all right. It probably won't harm us, but I'll have to turn off the torch. Quickly, behind this pillar.'

They stood still, flat against the wall. The small of Sharon's back tingled, as though there was something creeping up behind her. But she could feel the cold stone pressing against her and knew there was nothing there. She peered round the pillar into the darkness. Molecules of dust swam before her eyes, microscopic pin-pricks of light that formed shapes she could only dimly make out. They seemed to cluster around one bigger shape, gradually creating its outline. Now her eyes were getting used to the dark and the shape was becoming clearer. It was heading straight for her. It towered above her and a large clawed hand slowly reached out. She closed her eyes.

'So!' Feer, the leader of the Howen, snarled through his huge yellow teeth. Saliva spattered Diz's clothes. 'So . . . *you* are responsible for the strange scent in the air. And what are you, eh? A boy? Like all the others? Another mouth to feed? Of no use to dog nor beast?'

Diz was trying desperately not to look scared. He was, of course, petrified. Two of the Howen held him tightly from behind. He stared up at Feer, at the terrifying creature in black pearled leather towering over him, the lightning symbol blazing on his helmet, the blue crystal prism dangling from his sleek neck, red eyes boring into his. What would this awful dog thing do to him? What was going to happen now? Diz pushed the thought to the back of his mind but it didn't want to stay there. The cut on his leg was beginning to throb. He felt wretched.

'Where are you from, boy?' asked Feer. 'How did you get here?'

'Yes,' Raffer echoed. 'How did you get here?'

Diz stared back at the dog face. 'I don't know. I got lost and found myself in a classroom.'

'You did, eh? And who were you with?' Feer demanded, his face close to Diz's.

'Who, boy?' Raffer prodded him with the long, thin bone he always carried.

It hurt. Diz gritted his teeth. He wouldn't tell them about his sister. 'No one.'

'Ha!' barked Raffer. 'He was with one of the Rebels,

47

but the other boy escaped. He must know where they are.'

'Do you, boy?'

'No, I don't.'

'I think you do.'

They were in the hall. About half the Howen were there; the Children had been put to bed. The two Howen behind Diz increased the pressure of their grip.

'Tell us', Feer went on, 'how you really got here.'

'We must know,' Raffer snarled, prodding him even harder and making him wince in pain. 'We must. We must.'

'Tell us,' Feer said, his voice ripe with sweetness, over-ripe. 'Tell us how you got here and we will let you go.'

Diz looked squarely at the beast. 'Why do you want to know?'

At that there was silence in the hall. The Howen who had crowded round, shuffling and sniffing, were suddenly still. As still as the space between heartbeats.

'Why?' Feer whispered, and brought his great paw up to Diz's chin. 'Why? So that we may find a way out of this hell, out of this cursed building. We must escape.' His voice grew louder, desperate. 'We *must* escape or we will die. We are getting older and slower. We are all male . . . If we die . . .'

Feer stopped. The silence hung heavily, uncertainly. Diz suddenly saw the great sadness that hid behind the Howen's eyes. He almost felt sorry for him. But if the Howen were trapped, then he was trapped too – and Sharon. Then another thought struck him. If there is a way out . . . the way we came in . . . and if the Howen followed it . . .

Summoning up his courage, he stared back at the dog. 'Then I'm trapped too. I don't know how I got here.'

'Ha!' the Howen barked. Diz jumped. 'You do know, boy. But I'll give you some time to think it over. In the dungeons. With the Prowler.' The Howen leader chuckled dangerously. 'You *will* tell us everything you know.'

Then Feer threw back his huge head and laughed. Diz was showered in an explosion of spittle. 'And if you don't tell . . .' He stopped laughing. 'We'll just tip you down the disposal chute.' At that he laughed even louder.

The Howen crowded closer, barking, yelping, howling. Diz tried to put his hands to his ears but his arms were held too firmly. Their breath stank in his nostrils. The world seemed to close in on him, the noise and the stench, until he could hardly breathe. At a signal from Feer, the two Howen dragged Diz through the crowd and down to the dungeons.

Feer looked over his pack and held up a paw for silence. Gradually they quietened down. 'Bull!' he commanded. The Howen fell back and Bull stepped forward. Feer's voice was even softer than normal. 'I have a little job for your pet,' he smiled. And his massive paw stroked Alice's hair, almost lovingly.

The sky is full of diamonds, reflecting an endless blue. It is bursting with sunshine so bright it hurts the eyes.

He lies flat against the emerald grass, which sways

49

rhythmically around the outline of his body. The grass sings with the music of a thousand tiny insects: ants, beetles, spiders, flies, grasshoppers. A beetle with a brilliant red back crawls across his face. He brushes it aside and sits up. He feels the breeze blowing his hair, cool on his skin. There, at the bottom of the hill, his mother is beating a carpet that hangs on the rope line. All the colours are bright and true: the sky, the grass, the beetle, the green and purple patterns on the carpet, his mother's red hair. She calls him loudly, as though he is lost, but she must be able to see him quite clearly.

'Jaro! Jaro! Come and help me get this carpet in.'

Jaro runs down the hill towards her. He reaches her and buries his face in the folds of her skirt. It is damp, he realizes, from his tears. He is filled with sadness, there, buried in his mother's warm, friendly smell. He is crying now. He looks up from the skirt and sees only darkness.

'Are you all right?' a soft, gentle voice asks.

'Yes,' he whispers.

'Did you have that dream again?' Bel asks.

Jaro nods in the darkness. Bel senses this, reaches out a hand and holds his shoulder gently, softly rocking it. 'Don't worry,' she says quietly, soothing. 'It won't go on for ever. We'll get away soon, I can feel it. Just go back to sleep.'

'I'm all right,' Jaro whispers. 'Thanks.'

'Night, night.'

'Goodnight.'

Jaro lies in the darkness. Around him the Children sleep peacefully, huddled together on the floor under threadbare grey blankets. He gazes up at the ceiling. Beyond the ceiling, he thinks, the attic and the mice. Beyond that . . . who knows? The blue sky? Yes, the blue sky. He is sure of it. He feels beneath his pillow for the comfort of the small wooden box the boy dropped and grasps it.

He falls into sleep – and into the tall green grass beneath taller blue skies.

CHAPTER 6

BETRAYED

The beast known as the Prowler stood an arm's length from Sharon and the two Brethren hiding in the cellar's shadows. Sharon held her breath, standing as still as marble. She could feel the heat from it. She knew that its arm was poised above her like a boulder about to fall. She could smell its oily scent. And as she stood in the fearful darkness that was spreading through her like ink through blotting paper, a piece of jigsaw puzzle began to click into place.

Click!

The claw dragged along the wall above Sharon's head. Surely . . .

Click!

It changed direction, now scraping along the ceiling, dislodging motes of dust that Sharon could only feel, not see. The arm withdrew and the Prowler moved on. Slowly. Purposefully.

Click!

Then it was gone, swallowed up by the darkness.

The mice stepped back into the passageway and Reginald turned on the torch, keeping the beam pointed down. Nigel gave Sharon's arm a friendly squeeze. She smiled for him, her fear slowly evaporating as she brushed the dust from her shoulders.

'About the Prowler –' Sharon began.

'Not now, later,' Reginald said. 'We must hurry.' And they were on their way again. Now it was Nigel's turn to scout ahead. He disappeared into the darkness.

Very soon they came upon another flight of steps leading up. They waited for a few moments until Nigel reappeared. 'It's all right,' he said cheerfully. 'There's nobody about.'

The stairs spiralled. They were wooden, narrow and worn. The walls were grubby from the touch of a thousand hands – and paws. There was a distinctive smell that reminded Sharon of something, though she couldn't think what. Part of it was missing; an element that should have been there, but wasn't.

The stairs were steep and Sharon was quite puffed by the time they had climbed them all, although the mice didn't seem breathless in the least; not even Nigel, who had made the climb up and back once already. At the top there was light. Brighter than any Sharon had seen so far. She blinked. They were in a hallway, standing before three doors. It definitely reminded Sharon of the hall outside the school office.

'We're on the main level again now,' Nigel said. 'But you can only reach this place by going through the cellars.'

'If you don't mind,' Reginald said, 'we'll wait here.'

'It's not that we're scared,' Nigel joined in, 'not scared at all.'

'No,' said Reginald. 'It's just that it's, well, unhealthy in there.'

'Not scary – unhealthy,' Nigel added.

Sharon looked at the doors rather dubiously. 'Is it dangerous, then?' she asked.

'Oh no,' Reginald said, his whiskers twitching. 'The Howen send children in to collect the paper and it's never hurt a child.'

Nigel reached forward to open the middle door.

For a moment Sharon thought she was back at school. It was a flash of *déjà-vu*, the feeling that she'd lived that exact moment before and was about to live it again – and that she should *know* what was going to happen next, but couldn't quite remember. That smell, a mixture of peppermints and sweaty perfume, the smell of Mrs Mulligan, the school secretary. If she knocked on the door would Goony's sharp, shrill voice beckon her in?

Hesitantly, Nigel opened the door and stood back for Sharon to enter. She didn't know why but at that moment she really didn't want to go in. She wanted to turn around and go back down the stairs. She felt scared, even though she could see that the room beyond was nothing like the school office.

'Will you come in with me?' she asked Reginald. He shook his head. 'Please?'

Reginald smiled nervously. 'Well . . .'

'Yes, you go,' Nigel said quickly. 'I'll stay out here and keep guard.'

The room was dim after the brightly lit hallway outside, and bare. The walls, ceiling and floor were smooth, dull black. Everything was bathed in an eerie, pale-blue glow from the room's only source of light, a huge triangular television screen which dominated the opposite wall. A tiny white dot passed continually across it from right to left.

In the centre of the room there was a huge computer console. Its keyboard was dark blue and it had an odd organic look to it, as though it had grown from the floor. It was laid out in three sections which reminded Sharon of lily pads, but ugly lily pads that could never produce a beautiful flower.

'So this is the Big Cheese, is it?'

'It is,' Reginald said in a slightly awed voice. 'It's a machine of some kind, isn't it?'

'Yes, it is,' Sharon laughed.

'Have you ever seen one before?'

Well, thought Sharon, it is weird, but at last here is something I can understand. 'It's called a computer,' she said, 'although it's bigger than any I've ever seen before.' She studied the keyboard intently. The keys themselves were larger than normal, triangular and slightly concave. Each of the three sections had about thirty of them.

Reginald stood on tiptoe to see. 'Do you recognize any of the symbols on it?' he asked.

'They're letters of some kind,' Sharon muttered, 'although there are a lot I don't understand.' She tapped what she guessed might be the Return key.

'Yeeow!' she squealed, jerking her hand away. Both Reginald and Nigel jumped.

'What happened?' Reginald asked.

'It's all right. It gave me an electric shock.' Sharon sucked her tingling finger. 'Only a mild one. I just wasn't expecting it, that's all.' She glared at the computer. Then a thought struck her. 'Are we safe here? What if the Howen come?'

'Don't worry,' Nigel said. 'They never do. Like I said, they're scared of it. Not like us. They wait at the bottom and send a couple of the Children up. They keep some children as pets you know, grant them favours.'

Sharon shivered.

'That's the slot where the paper comes out,' Reginald pointed. 'The Children collect it and take it to the Howen for sorting.'

'Oh yeah,' Sharon said, remembering their earlier conversation. 'I'd like to see some of the paper. I might be able to read it. What happens to it after that?'

'It goes down the waste-disposal chute.'

'Oh.' There was disappointment in her voice.

'Perhaps we *can* get hold of some,' Reginald said.

Sharon examined the computer – keeping well away from it. What would happen if I unplugged it? She wondered. But she couldn't see any sign of a plug, or even an on/off switch.

'Someone's coming,' Nigel hissed.

'Quick!' Reginald whispered, and hustled her from the room. They went through the right-hand door, leaving it slightly ajar. They were in a store cupboard. Sharon could faintly make out the empty shelves all around them.

The footsteps that Nigel's sensitive ears had picked up could be heard easily now, slowly climbing the stairs. In a moment they were outside the door.

Reginald, who was squinting through the crack, breathed a sigh of relief and swung the door open.

The boy jumped in surprise. Then he grinned. 'Hello,' he said, 'we've been looking for you lot.'

Sharon and the Brethren stepped out.

'You must be Diz's sister.'

Sharon found Nigel's arm and squeezed it hopefully. 'Is Diz all right?' she demanded of the boy. 'Is he safe? Do you know where he is?'

'No, I don't. But I have to take you to my friends. Then maybe we can find some way of rescuing him.'

Sharon looked at the mice and then back to the boy, suddenly unsure of what to say.

'We must have a meeting,' the boy told the mice. 'Can you all be at the Old Stairway at breakfast-time?'

'Most certainly,' Reginald said. He held Sharon's hand. 'Don't worry. Together we will surely rescue your brother.' He turned back to the boy. 'Look after her.'

'You can depend on it.'

'Chin up,' Nigel said. Then the Brethren left, making no noise at all as they scampered down the wooden stairs and disappeared into the darkness.

Sharon looked at the boy. Although he was smiling with his mouth, his eyes were cold and unfriendly and would not directly meet her gaze. He was taller than her, very thin, with a straggly mop of red hair.

'What's your name?' she asked.

'They call me Ginger.'

Diz sat slumped on a wooden box, leaning against the wall. He was in a small room somewhere in the cellars, the Howen's captive. They had given him a blanket, greasy and grey, even though it wasn't cold. It lay in a heap where they'd thrown it. Perhaps there was a tiny spark of compassion in the Howen somewhere, he thought. He remembered the sadness he'd seen in Feer's eyes.

A dim light came from a tiny disc set in the wall. The room was whitewashed, but dingy; the door was locked. Diz sat, feeling miserable and alone, and thought back over his extraordinary day. He wondered what time it was. He supposed it must be around bedtime. He certainly felt tired – physically and mentally exhausted. His mother would be sick with worry. But what could he do? He could hardly have anticipated all this and left her a note. Dear Mum, I won't be home tonight as I'm going to be captured by giant dogs who'll probably kill me. Neither will Sharon as she'll be captured by mice. Don't worry. Love Diz.

It upset him to think of his mother worrying. She was only just getting over Dad going. He had never really understood why his dad had left. It wasn't as if he or Mum quarrelled much and Dad didn't have another woman. He had a girlfriend now, though. She liked to be called Auntie Rose, but Diz always called her Rosie for a laugh. She didn't like that. She was OK, he supposed. His dad liked her, anyway.

He smiled to himself, but the picture of Rose in his mind faded, to be replaced by Feer's gruesome head, his eyes full of malice this time, and Diz shuddered. He was a prisoner of the Howen. He might never see his mum or dad or Rose or even Sharon again. It was crazy. He wanted nothing more to do with it. If this was an adventure story he was in, then he wanted to close the book right now and go home.

And where was Sharon?

'Oh no!' He leapt from the box in alarm. There was a great big spider crawling across it. He hated spiders and this one was a giant. He watched it for a few moments, his heart beating madly. He hated to do this, but he felt he had no real choice in the matter. He knocked it off the box with his outstretched foot and stood on it.

No ...

Diz leapt back and stared at the squidgy mess. Had he imagined it? Had the spider cried out? Of course not. But here in this crazy place, anything was possible.

It was no good. He would have to get some sleep. He took off his school jacket, brushed off the dust and dirt half-heartedly with his hand and rolled it up for a pillow. He put it down some way from the dead spider; killing it had unsettled him.

Now he needed a pee. Diz went over to the door and banged. No response. He banged the door again and shouted. Still nothing. He could wait no longer; he'd have to go in the corner.

There was no light switch in the room. He'd have to sleep with the light on. Just as well, really – there might be more spiders about. He didn't think he'd be able to doze off, anyway. Diz wrapped himself in the blanket, lay down and fell asleep almost immediately.

The Rebels sat around their leader, Els. They had sorted out their new headquarters at Far Point and moved in their few precious belongings. Now, before going to sleep, they were going to discuss the day's events; in particular, the appearance of the newcomers.

Far Point was a narrow, squashed-up room, being, as the name suggested, the nearest to the Edge that anyone had been able to explore. It was the only room in that part of the building able to accommodate them all. They sat around, huddled together in their few blankets, chewing scraps of greyroot and listening to what Els had to say.

'Things are happening. Unusual things. And they seem to revolve around these new children. Now they may merely be trapped here like us, but I feel somehow there's more to it than that.'

She looked at the others, hoping for a response. Nobody spoke. She continued. 'It seems to me that the first thing we should do tomorrow is try to rescue Diz. Then we must contact the Brethren and find his sister, Sharon.'

'Why?' asked Baloney. 'And what about finding food? Shouldn't we do that first? The greyroot's nearly all gone.' Several of the Rebels were nodding in agreement. They were hungry.

'We have to rescue Diz,' Els said, 'for the reasons I've said before. I think Diz and Sharon can help us. And anyway, we can't let the Howen have him. It was our fault they got him in the first place.' They all looked at her guiltily. 'Well?'

Moke spoke up. 'I agree. Diz is OK. He's a friend now. I was nearly caught with him, you know. We have to help him somehow.'

'Listen,' Els said. 'First thing tomorrow we'll divide into two groups. Baloney can take one group and organize a food hunt and Moke and I will take the other and try to work out a plan or something to rescue Diz. We'll get on to the Brethren, too.'

'Do we know she's with them?' asked Moke.

'She must be. The Howen would have her by now otherwise. Well, does that sound all right to everyone?'

They all nodded in agreement. Els felt pleased. But there was something wrong. Something was missing. Of course, there was one person who always disagreed with everything she said. Where was Ginger? Oh well, they'd worry about him in the morning. She didn't care that much about him; he could look after himself, she was sure.

The Rebels set their guard, lay on the floor and covered themselves in blankets. They were all soon asleep.

Ginger was leading Sharon to the Howen, although she didn't know that yet. He didn't think Els should be the leader of their group and he disliked girls in general. The Howen would be pleased to have this one. They would certainly reward him. She was holding grimly to his arm as he led her, half-running, through the unlit passages in the cellars. He was smiling wickedly to himself.

'Must we go so fast?' Sharon panted.

He didn't answer. Instead he increased the pace.

At last they reached some stairs and went up. Although Sharon knew the main passages of the building were more dangerous, she much preferred to be in the light. After all, she had been safe so far. The Brethren, and presumably the Rebels too, seemed to know how to avoid the Howen. And a meeting between the Brethren and the Rebels had been agreed. Maybe things weren't so black after all. If only Ginger would slow down. She was getting out of breath.

They turned a corner into a long corridor. One of the Howen was walking towards them. Sharon twisted around, ready to run back. But, to her horror, Ginger gripped her arm tightly and continued onwards. She could see he was grinning. What was going on? Was he mad? She struggled but he held her even tighter. In desperation she kicked him. He yelled in pain, slipped, and for a moment his grip loosened. She leapt free, turned and ran blindly back along the maze of corridors. But Ginger recovered his balance and she could hear him behind her. She was out of breath and all the time Ginger and the Howen were getting closer; she could hear their footsteps echoing through the strangely quiet building.

She reached a dead end. Panic.

Searching desperately, Sharon saw a small door in the wall and yanked it open. It led to some kind of chute. She would have to risk it; Ginger was about to round the corner. She dived through the door and it thudded shut behind her, like a mouth closing. She slid down the chute and the dark swallowed her.

Bartholomew and Jeroboam stood each side of the Game of Changes, staring at the pieces, thinking intently about the different moves that might be made, and which would be the right one.

They had set up the Game when they first arrived in the building. It had occupied all their time for the first few months – finding wood for the pieces, shaping them with their sharp teeth, fashioning a board. Marking the board had posed the greatest problem. In the end they had used their own blood as paint. So the Game had been made with their blood and their skills.

Time passed differently for the Brethren than for the building's other inhabitants. Most of their days were spent meditating. Then the usually cramped attic would seem to expand into a huge emptiness, a vast space of great loneliness and beauty. Time itself would slow down. And after meditation, the Game would come into sharp focus and the Brethren would contemplate their moves.

Now the Game seemed to be nearing a solution. But it could still go in one of two ways. Jeroboam looked long and hard at Bartholomew. Then he nodded. They had decided. Bartholomew reached forward, lifted the heavy wooden piece, and moved it.

CHAPTER 7

BREAKFAST

Jaro lay on the hillside beneath the hot sun and deep-blue sky, his eyes closed. He listened contentedly to the summer sounds of insects moving busily through the long grass. He was hungry. He thought he might run down the hill to ask his mother what was for breakfast. He felt an insect alight on his cheek and crawl towards his ear. It made a loud, shrill noise.

peep!

He brushed the insect aside. It must have landed near his ear because it made the noise again, more loudly this time.

peep!

In fact it repeated the sound over and over again.

peep!
peep!
peep!
peeeeeeeeeeeeeeeeeeeeeeeeeeeeeeeeep!

He heard his mother calling him.

'Jaro, Jaro, wake up.'

He opened his eyes. Of course there was no sun, just the dull electric light; no hill, just the dormitory, the claustrophobic smells of sleep and sweat; and Bel shaking him.

He was hungry, but he knew what was for breakfast. Greyroot.

Wearily he sat up, tossed his blanket aside and felt for his shirt.

'Do you think I'll ever see my mother again?' he asked Bel. He found the shirt and pulled it on.

Bel finished tidying their blankets. Thoughtfully she smoothed the folds and creases in her long shirt. 'Of course,' she said. She put her arms around his skinny shoulders, holding her warmth to his, and gave him a hug. 'Come on or we'll miss breakfast.'

'I hope it's that yummy greyroot,' Jaro said. Then they both smiled and together joined the line of sleepy children making their way to the canteen. Had Jaro glanced back, he would have seen the box of matches, left lying by the blankets in full view on the floor.

A sky full of smoke. The smell of sulphur. Tall mountains the colour of soot and fire. A few sorrowful trees, stunted and bent with singed branches and a few blackened leaves.

Nigel followed the Brethren as they wound their way through narrow pathways cut into the volcanic rock. He was going home. He was weary and hungry but determined. Now he was becoming excited, impatient almost. Home was just over the next mountain.

The pathway led to a large stone building. Nigel knew there was food inside – nuts, grain, great rolls of spiced and seeded bread – but Reginald the Abbot was standing at the door, barring their way. Nigel and the other Brethren begged him to let them pass. He shook his head, then raised a peculiar, star-shaped whistle to his mouth and blew a series of short sharp notes followed by one long one.

peep!
peep!
peep!
peep!
peep!
peeeeeeeeeeeeeeeeeeeeeeeeeeeeeeeeeep!

Nigel woke up. Blasted pips, he thought. Wake me up every morning. And always when I'm nearly home . . .

He glanced at the other Brethren, huddled in the gloom. It was his task to prepare breakfast. Stepping lightly over his companions, he made his way to the greyroot store.

Greyroot was the one thing that linked all the sections of this strange community – the Brethren, the Howen, the Children, the Rebels. It was their chief source of nourishment. Originally the creeper-like plant had grown only in the central quadrangle, but now it surfaced in all sorts of odd places. Often, whole plants would wither and die, to be replaced by new growth elsewhere. The Brethren had tried to cultivate it in the attic but had failed. It never grew in the dark cellar spaces, either. It seemed to need light; if only the dim electric light found chiefly on the main level of the building.

Greyroot was not completely grey but had a green tinge to it. It looked unappetizing and it was just that, tasting like a mixture of cabbage and sawdust. Grey-fruit, which seemed to follow no season but simply appeared on the greyroot plant when it felt like it, resembled a small, tough pear. It was sweeter than its parent plant but just as uninviting.

Although lacking in some vitamins, greyroot was apparently good for you. But there wasn't enough of it for the building's community. And, served up every day, it was very, very boring.

Diz, locked in a small, dingy room in the cellars, was tasting greyroot for the first time. He hoped it would be the last. It was like eating raw cabbage that crumbled in his mouth. He washed it down with a mug of cold water.

He took a good look at the girl who had brought him his breakfast. She had appeared soon after the pips had woken him up. School pips; he might have guessed. She was about his age, smaller than he was, with delicate features and long, wispy brown hair. Her eyes were bright and blue. Her voice was soft. She said her name was Alice.

He felt sweaty, sticky, dirty, smelly and still hungry. His leg ached.

'How did you get here?' she asked.

'The Howen locked me in, of course.'

'No,' she said, 'not in this room. How did you get into the building?'

67

'How did you?'

Her voice became even softer. 'I can't remember. None of us can, properly. I remember being warm and snug and seeing a kind face with a big smile and being lifted high up in the sunshine . . .' Her voice trailed away to nothing. She just stood gazing at Diz, as though he were a hundred miles away. She looked very sad to Diz. It made him feel uncomfortable.

'We came through the attic from our school,' he said, to break the silence. 'I don't understand how. Some kind of time warp? Like Doctor Who perhaps.' He shrugged.

'Doctor Who?' she asked, looking at him blankly.

For a second Diz thought that might have been a joke. 'No matter,' he said.

'Who were you with?' she asked.

'My sister, Sharon.'

Wait a minute, Diz thought to himself. I don't know anything about this girl. Why did she bring me breakfast? Who made me the breakfast? The Howen . . . I must have assumed she was on our side because she's one of the Children but . . .

'Why do you want to know?' he asked Alice.

'I'm just interested, that's all.' She half-smiled but avoided his gaze. 'It's exciting. Nothing new has happened here since I can remember. It's so boring.'

Diz felt sorry for her, but he mustn't tell her anything, just in case. 'Look,' he said gently, 'I really don't know how we got here. I only know that there must be some way out and we're going to try to help you find it.'

She nodded, smiled and, still without meeting his

gaze, picked up the empty bowl and went out. He heard a key turn in the lock.

He stared morosely at the closed door. It had a small window cut in the top with two iron bars across. A prison within a prison, he thought. The girl, I should have asked her things, tried to find out more. And who am I to tell her I can find the way out. I haven't got a clue. I wasn't thinking, either. I could easily have escaped then.

He went over to the door and rattled it angrily.

Sharon woke in the dark. She must have somehow snuggled right down in the covers, but it felt all wrong. Where was she? This wasn't her duvet. She realized she was trapped underground and a wave of panic arose. This wasn't her bedroom. Why was there no light? Then she remembered.

It was as though she was in a tiny room. She could feel the walls and ceiling by stretching out her hand. They felt soft. Her bed felt soft, too, but very lumpy. Her back ached. She was thirsty. And hungry. Her bladder was full. She would have to move.

She tunnelled her way out of her makeshift sleeping quarters into the weak light of the room. Last night was coming back to her. She shivered. She remembered the chase and sliding down what was obviously a laundry chute into this room. The panic – and then willing herself to be calm, to quieten down and try to gather her wits. Ginger and the Howen hadn't followed her at any rate. They probably didn't know where the chute went (at least, she hoped not).

She'd found herself in a storeroom of some kind.

She'd tried the door. It was locked. Piled against one wall, but filling half the room were hundreds of blue roller towels, packed with boards between them at regular intervals. She'd been able to rearrange them and had made herself a kind of nest. In other circumstances, she'd thought, this could have been fun. She'd unrolled one for a mattress, climbed into the tunnel she'd made and fallen asleep.

Now Sharon looked around the storeroom. There was a bad smell. An old, mouldy smell. Mentally she ticked off the things she must do. One – have a pee. Two – find something to eat and drink. Three – find a way out of the room. How do you open a locked door without a key? Four – wash. She felt filthy, caked in grime and sweat. She must smell terrible. Five – find the Brethren, or the Rebels.

Oh no! Ginger had set up a meeting between the Rebels and the Brethren for this morning. But Ginger had led her straight to the Howen. He was a traitor. That meant one thing: the meeting was a trap. But how could she warn the Brethren? She couldn't.

Sharon began to feel disheartened. It was all too much. Was it even tomorrow yet? She had no way of knowing. Her body told her yes, but she couldn't rely on that. She remembered her dad telling her about the day he'd got up two hours too early and cycled the four kilometre to the mill. He'd wondered where all the familiar faces were, the people he saw on the way to work at that time every morning. When he arrived he found out his mistake. But how could she find out the time? It might still be the middle of the night.

She looked around at the boxes and cartons piled

up against the walls, hoping for inspiration. She tore one of the smaller packages open. Candles. No help, but they might prove useful later on. She stuffed a handful in her jacket pocket. There was a large wooden chest in one corner of the room. The mouldy smell hung all around it. Gingerly she heaved up the lid. She shrieked in fear and suprise, and leapt back, nearly tripping over some boxes.

The smell filled the room. The chest was full of clothes, ripe with mould. Large, soft, yellow maggots were crawling all over them.

Sharon rushed back to the door. Then she noticed that the handle of a broom was jamming it shut; it wasn't locked at all. She pulled the broomhead from behind a crate and dislodged it, then she yanked the door open and fell retching into the next room.

Light spilled through and Sharon could make out white tiles covering the floor and walls. The room was a tangle of pipes and it was very warm. In one corner was a huge boiler, from behind which she could hear the low hum of electricity, and along one wall were three huge, white enamel sinks.

She tried one of the sink's taps: water gushed out. It looked all right. Neither the Howen, the Children, nor the Brethren would have been able to survive without water, she figured, and she tasted it. Cold and sweet.

There were two other doors in the room. One led to a dark corridor. Behind the other was a small cubicle. A lavatory.

Oh joy.

The Brethren had eaten well. Greyroot agreed with

their constitutions even though it was boring. They were walking to the Old Stairway for their meeting with the Rebels, as arranged by Ginger. They were unaware of Sharon's adventure.

They were also unaware that ten Howen, led by Feer, were waiting for them round the next corner.

CHAPTER 8

REUNION

In the Rebels' hideout, Els, Moke, Ginger and Crab were holding a council of war. The other Rebels had left to find food. Els had asked Ginger where he'd been last night and he'd said he was looking for a new patch of greyroot, one that the Brethren had told him about. It had seemed feasible to Els. She had no reason to suspect otherwise. Now they were planning Diz's rescue.

'If he's still captive,' Els said, 'he'll be in one of the dungeons. We'll have to find which one and get him out.'

'But there's always Howen in that area,' Moke replied. 'It'll be dangerous.'

'Why don't we create a diversion?' Els suggested. 'You know, give them something else to think about.'

'That's a good idea,' Moke agreed. 'But what?'

They all sat deep in thought.

'You know what?' said Crab.

'What?' Els inquired.

'I like Diz.'

'Me, too,' Els said. 'Me, too.'

*

Sharon felt much better now. She had washed as best she could in the cold water (there were plenty of towels) and she had shaken some of the dust out of her clothes. Now she had to find the Brethren and some food.

She made her way quietly along the dark cellar corridor, listening intently for sounds of the Howen or the Prowler. By now she was pretty sure she knew what the Prowler was. But she wished she could figure out what this building was and how she and Diz had come to be here. And, more importantly, how they could escape.

Then she heard voices.

She peered round the next corner and gasped in surprise. Weak light from a small barred window cut in the top of a door filtered into the passage. By the door, but out of sight of the window, stood one of the Howen. He was short and stocky, dressed in a leather tunic and a thick leather collar, both studded with iron spikes. He had the look of a bulldog. He was holding a wicked, iron-spiked club.

Sharon strained her ears. Yes. She recognized one of the voices. Her heart leapt and she felt giddy with relief. Diz. Diz. Diz. She'd found him. She leant back against the wall round the corner and out of sight, her heart thumping madly.

She peered round the corner again. The door opened and more light briefly lit the gloom. A girl stepped out of the room, closed the door and locked it behind her. The girl and the Howen disappeared into the darkness.

Sharon waited a few moments until she was sure

they'd gone, until she could bear the waiting no longer. Suddenly she heard the door being rattled. For a second she was uncertain what to do, then she ran over to the door. On tiptoe she could just see through the barred window. There was Diz, with his back to her.

'Dizzy,' Sharon whispered.

Diz spun round. For a moment he looked blank; then he realized who it was. Sharon. She was alive. She was all right. He grabbed the box, hauled it across to the door and stood on it.

'It's really you! You're OK. I didn't think I'd ever see you again.'

They held hands through the gaps between the bars.

'You haven't got a key, I suppose?' Diz asked hopefully. 'They've locked me in.'

'No ... I'm sorry. It's so good to see you. I heard you being caught.'

Sharon told Diz all that had happened to her since they'd been separated.

'You haven't met the Howen yet, then?' Diz said.

'Not up close. I saw the one in the classroom and the one outside here.'

'They're horrible. They're huge and they slobber and their breath stinks. I've *got* to get out of here. They're going to tip me down the waste-disposal chute.'

'I'll try to get to the Rebels or the Brethren. They'll help. They might even have a key.'

'Talk to Moke, he's all right. Look, let's try and work all this out. We can't be trapped here for ever.

There *must* be a way out. What do we know about this place?'

Sharon thought for a moment. All the time she was half-listening down the corridor in case anybody or anything came. Darkness swirled around her. Her brother was safe. She was touching him. But he could be taken away again at any moment.

'Hmmm. Let's see. We're in some kind of building, very much like our own school, but much, much bigger. There are no exits to the outside, or even outside windows. The whole place is lit by electricity. And there's water. And a plant that everybody eats.'

'It tastes like Dad's socks.'

'I know. . . . What else. . . . There's an office. I thought it was going to be Goony's but it's not. It just feels like it. There's a giant computer in it with this big triangular screen and a white dot going across it.'

'A computer!' Diz interrupted excitedly. 'A big computer? And it's up and running?'

'Yes, the Brethren call it the Big Cheese. The Howen –'

'That's it. Something must be controlling all this. Buildings don't just power themselves, do they? It's the computer.'

'Everyone seems scared of it. The Howen have got the Children sifting through the print-out. It doesn't mean anything to them, of course. I don't think they can even read.'

'The print-out's probably not important anyway,' Diz said. 'What we've got to do is to get into the computer. Get into its programs.'

'Yes, I know. But how? It gave me an electric shock when I touched it.'

There was a noise from the darkness.

'I must go,' Sharon whispered. 'Someone's coming. Don't worry.' The approaching footsteps were clear now. 'Good luck!'

'Sharon . . .' Diz whispered after her. But she was gone.

The Brethren made their way through the dark, winding cellar passageways, on their way to meet the Rebels. Or so they thought. They felt reasonably safe in this part of the cellars and were not taking their usual precautions. When Gladly ran ahead to check around the next corner he was not really expecting to come face to face with ten Howen in full battle-dress – and so he stopped and just stood there, staring.

Staring at the Howen – at their armour of leather and iron spikes, at their swords and spiked clubs, at their teeth and slobbering mouths and at their wild, red eyes, glowing with blood and fire. Gladly's limbs were frozen; he wanted to move but he couldn't. Time seemed to slow down and stop. Gladly and the Howen faced one another.

Then a great roaring howl snapped him out of the trance. He turned and bolted, crashing through the Brethren like a gale through sheets of paper. 'Run! Run! HOWEN!'

The other Brethren reacted immediately. They turned and fled.

The Howen were stronger and faster than the Brethren. Had they been racing across an open field the Howen would have won, no contest. But in the dark, twisting, underground passages beneath the building, the odds were almost in the Brethren's favour. Almost, but not quite.

The long passageway turned sharply. The Brethren were round the corner in no time and off into the darkness. The Howen hit the corner like a herd of elephants on a children's slide. Two of them fell and it took them several seconds to recover. But they were soon back in pursuit. Feer leading, his great head nearly as high as the ceiling. Their howls echoed like a train in a tunnel.

The corridor forked. The Brethren could no longer be seen, but even Feer's diminished sense of smell could pick up their sharp scent of fear. He let out another great howl as he led his pack into the darkness.

The Brethren were very fast over short distances but they were already beginning to tire. Gladly, who had been at the front, was now trailing. Another branching of the ways. They turned left. Gladly's legs ached, he was breathing in great gasps. They ran on, the cries of the Howen loud in their ears.

The Howen took the next corner more carefully. At last, the thought burned through Feer's mind, we shall have the mice. Roasted. Fried. Barbecued . . . The scent was vibrant, mouth-watering. The Brethren could not escape. They were running towards the main staircase. If they tried to run up it . . . if they even reached that far . . .

'What now?' Nigel panted. 'We can't out-run them.'

'This way,' Reginald ordered.

They turned down a narrow passage, forcing their legs forward. It was a tight squeeze; they had to run in single file.

'That should slow them a bit,' Reginald gasped. They were stumbling down a large corridor beneath the main rooms now. 'It should be here somewhere,' Reginald was muttering. 'Ah, yes . . .'

The Brethren stopped. They could hear the Howen moaning and complaining as they followed Feer's great bulk, squeezing through the narrow passage. But within seconds they would come.

'Run ahead a little way and flatten yourselves against the wall.' Good old Reginald. He had a plan. The other Brethren moved quickly forward and hugged the wall.

Reginald slid the torch from its pocket, turned it on and laid it on the ground, facing the darkness. He hoped this would work. Then he scampered across the corridor to join the others.

Feer appeared, reached for the torch and picked it up. But, just as the other Howen joined him, a massive shape materialized from the darkness and a great, metal claw reached for the torch in Feer's grasp. The other nine Howen cowered behind their leader, mesmerized by the gigantic beast blocking their way.

The Howen were not noted for their bravery but Feer was an exception. He swung his sword at the creature with all his might. It bounced off with a deafening clang and spun from Feer's grip. The metal claw inched closer to the torch.

Feer's nerve broke. He turned and ran. The other Howen followed. Behind the Prowler, out of sight, the Brethren crept away.

Diz was tied to a wooden chair. It had a curved back

and was very uncomfortable. The Howen had taken him from the dungeon and brought him to this room. It reminded him of the school staffroom. In the corner some moth-eaten, mouldy armchairs had been piled up. Before him stood Raffer, Feer's lieutenant.

'Do you know what's through that door?' Raffer asked, his voice as soft as chalk dust, pointing with his long, ornamental bone to a door at the back of the room.

Diz shook his head. The Howen grinned, showing his blackened teeth and pink gums.

'The waste-disposal chute.' Raffer's grin became a chuckle. 'And that's where you're going, boy. Down the chute. Do you know what's down the chute? Nothing but rubbish. Nowhere. Goodbye. Down with the rubbish, eh, Diz? Unless . . .'

He playfully prodded Diz's chin with the bone.

'Unless, boy,' Raffer said again, 'unless you give us some information.'

Diz stared at him with as much defiance as he could muster. What could he possibly tell this creature? He tried to think of Sharon, to keep his mind from what was happening to him. At least *she* was safe.

Raffer walked around Diz, his bone never very far from Diz's head. 'We know you came here through the attic. We know you came with your sister. We'll capture her soon, you know. We may even have her already. All you have to do is show us the way out.'

Still Diz was silent. Should he tell them about the computer, he wondered. But no, why should he? He wasn't going to help these loathsome creatures. The Howen's soft voice was getting louder.

'It's hopeless, boy. You've got no chance. We have the Brethren, you know. Soon we'll have the Rebels, as sure as bones are bones. Then we'll have your sister. She can't last out on her own. And you'll be dead. Dumped into oblivion.' His voice was now a growl. He brought his face down to Diz's.

'Tell us how to get out of here and you can go free. The whole blasted lot of you can go free. We don't want you. We don't care.' He was shouting now. Wild.

Diz was shaking. He clenched his teeth. He'd tell them nothing.

Then the door crashed open and there stood Feer. He was trembling with rage, and he was holding a frightened boy by the scruff of the neck. It was Ginger.

CHAPTER 9

IN THE DARK

Baloney and the food party had returned to the hideout empty-handed and the Rebels were in a gloomy and apathetic mood. They were hungry. There had been many times like this in the past. Often they went for three or four days without anything to eat. Then they would discover a new patch of greyroot and all would be well.

Els didn't like this mood. It was the sheer boredom of their existence that got to her the most. Now at last they had something to do, something other than just moping about, trying to keep out of the Howen's way. But here were the so-called Rebels sitting around moaning, while their chances of rescuing Diz were lessening with every gloomy minute that crawled past.

'At least the Children eat regularly,' Baloney complained. 'At least they get their meals on time.'

'Oh.' Els turned on him, her voice loud and angry. 'So you'd rather go and live with the dogs, eh? You'd rather be bossed about all day and made to do stupid jobs, like looking at all that mumbo-jumbo stuff on the paper? You'd rather be beaten and whipped, eh? Well, go on then. Go back to 'em.'

'Look,' Baloney said, his voice trembling, 'I didn't mean that. It's just that I'm hungry, that's all.'

'Are we going to rescue Diz or not? Surely we're not pulling out because we're hungry, are we?' Els was cross.

'I agree with Els,' Moke said. 'At least doing something would be better than sitting around here feeling sorry for ourselves.'

At that moment Crab burst into the room. He had a big grin on his face. 'We've got a visitor.'

Sharon entered. She looked round at the Rebels, a relieved smile on her face. She was a little out of breath, but she'd made it at last. She'd been wandering around the cellars for what had seemed like hours before she'd met Crab.

The Rebels were smiling back at her, but their smiles were a little forced. They weren't quite as impressive as Sharon had expected; they looked so weary and downcast.

'I'm Moke. You must be Sharon.'

'And I'm Els, sort of the leader. We meet at last. Diz told us all about you.'

Sharon held out her hand. Els looked at it, not sure what this meant.

'We shake hands where I come from,' Sharon said. 'As a kind of friendly greeting.'

Els took her hand, awkwardly, then introduced Sharon to everyone and explained the reason for their glum faces. Sharon liked Els at once, and knew they would get on. Her smile was genuine, at least. As were Moke's and Crab's. She wasn't sure how they'd take the news of Ginger, though.

'It's about Ginger,' Sharon began. She didn't quite know how to put this. She would just have to say it all at once and hope it came out straight. 'I think . . . that is . . . he's a traitor.' And she told them all what Ginger had done.

She was surprised by how calmly they took it.

'It's no great shock to me,' Els said. 'He's been so argumentative lately, I thought something was up. Maybe he felt he could do some kind of deal with them.'

'He'll be lucky,' Moke said. 'I wouldn't trust them further than I could throw a stick with both hands tied behind my back.'

'I wonder where he is now,' Els mused. 'He was here just a minute ago. Did anyone see him go?'

The Rebels seemed to be livening up a bit now. They shook their heads.

'This means,' said Moke, 'that we're not safe here. He could be leading the Howen to us right now. We'll have to move again.'

There was general groaning.

'Well, before we rescue Diz, we'd better figure out where to make our next base. Anyone got any bright ideas?'

'Where is it?' Jaro was standing in the dormitory, holding a blanket helplessly. 'The box. It's gone.' He shook the blanket and threw it aside. Then he picked up his pillow, it thumped hard and hurled it across the room.

84

'What?' Bel asked. 'What's the matter? Why have we come back here? If the Howen find us . . .'

Jaro slumped to the floor. 'The box. That boy, the one the Howen were after. I had his little wooden box and now I've lost it. I must have left it here before breakfast.'

'Was it special, then?'

Jaro shook his head. 'I suppose not . . . It was just his, that's all.'

Bel put her hand on his shoulder to comfort him.

'Well,' she said, 'It was only a box . . .' She laughed and cuffed his arm. 'Maybe we should do it now. Escape. Shall we? Shall we look for the Rebels? It's a good time, while the Howen are busy with everything else going on.'

Jaro looked up and smiled softly. 'I'd like to. It won't be long, Bel. Then we will. I'd just like to think about it a bit longer. Soon we will, I promise.'

She lightly touched his hot cheek with her cool fingers and smiled.

They were not to know that soon the Rebels would be looking for them.

Feer stood over Diz, who was tied to the wooden chair in the staffroom, and dangled Ginger by the scruff of his neck.

'This is what we do to boys who try to double-cross us,' he growled. 'Boys who promise to help us and then run away at the last moment.'

'I didn't!' Ginger shrieked.

Feer crossed the staffroom in four long, angry strides, propelling the unfortunate Ginger before him.

At the door he turned and ordered Raffer to follow them. Diz heard, and felt, the door behind him slam shut, the door to the waste-disposal chute. Surely not . . . A draught of cold air threw an icy shiver up his spine.

For a short time, maybe for only four minutes, the Prowler had followed the heat trace of the fleeing Howen. But this was long enough to deflect the creature from the route it had followed for many years. Now it followed a new pathway through the labyrinthine cellars. And along this pathway the Prowler could sense food. Alert, as always, to movements, noises, it moved slowly on. Food. Energy. Sustenance. Closer now. Closer. Close.

Diz had lost all feeling in his hands. His arms were still tied to the chair and his captors had been gone for ages. He'd tried flexing his fingers and wrists, but the dull ache had finally given way to numbness.

He was worried now, he realized. More worried than at any time since he and Sharon had found themselves in this crazy place. Even his first glimpse of the Howen, which had been a terrifying shock, seemed like yesterday's fading dream. And up until now he hadn't really thought the Howen would hurt him. Not deep down. But seeing Ginger hauled through the room and taken down to the waste-disposal chute . . . It didn't bear thinking about. Now he finally understood that the Howen meant business.

Diz judged that this room was well-used by the Howen. A thin carpet of matted hair covered the filthy floor. There was a nasty smell, too, which came from the vicinity of the piled-up armchairs. What a dismal place. He couldn't think of one thing that had made him laugh since he'd been here.

On the wall facing him, level with the top of his head, was a shelf piled up with junk. He could see a pair of PE shorts, a notched stick, a water pistol, one grubby trainer, a football . . . and a spider.

A spider?

The spider moved.

Diz jumped. His blood froze. It was even bigger than the monster he had squashed last night. It's bound to ignore me, he thought; of course it will. They always do. It'll just go about its normal business of catching flies. But as though the spider could read his mind, it walked towards him across the junk on the shelf, each leg rising and falling in a slow-motion dance. At the edge it dropped slowly to the floor on a glittering silver thread. Like someone abseiling down a cliff, Diz thought.

He watched, fascinated, as the spider crawled towards him. He felt himself sweating. His mouth and lips were dry. The spider was slowly advancing across the floor, picking its way with great distaste over the hairs, as though understanding where they had come from.

Diz thought he would scream. The spider's body was the size of his fist; its legs were longer than his fingers. It was not black but a dark, woolly brown and it had eight tiny red eyes that seemed to fix him with a penetrating stare. He knew he must push the chair backwards, get away. But he couldn't move. All control of his body had deserted him.

The spider crawled on to his foot and he could feel the gentle tug on his trousers as it began to climb. He could feel the terror building. It was more than he could bear. *I'm sorry I killed that spider*, his mind shouted, as though it could make a difference. *I'm sorry. Please. No!*

Now the spider had reached his numb hand. There it stopped, still staring at Diz with its tiny red eyes. Brush it away! Brush it away! But he couldn't move his hands.

Calm down, Diz told himself. Getting into a panic isn't helping. Calm down. Deep breaths. In. Out. In. Out. Then, just as he felt he was getting hold of the situation, that maybe the spider wouldn't bite him if he was still and quiet and offered no threat, he noticed something that flipped his whole world upside-down.

The spider wore a belt. And from that belt hung a small silver sword.

From within the great body of the Prowler – whose skin once shone like a polished mirror but was now dulled with dust, dirt and grime – an arm appeared, moving slowly towards the source of energy, its next meal: the glowing electric disc on the ceiling. The Prowler had two metal rods rather than a hand and these smashed the disc, cascading glass and filament in a glittering shower.

The two rods connected with the socket and power surged into the Prowler at last. Its batteries, run-down, nearly dead, drank the electricity eagerly, feeling their cells filling with the life-giving juice. Dials spun. Lights flashed. The Prowler filled his being with fuel and began to hum with vibrant power as long-dead circuits received the kiss of life.

Now lights in the building began to flicker. Hidden generators were having problems coping with this sudden drain on the energy supply. Finally, the Prowler's demands became too great and fuses began to blow. The whole building was plunged into darkness.

In the staffroom, the spider drew the silver sword from its scabbard, still holding Diz's gaze with his own.

The spider spoke.

'Are you the boy who killed Hari ?'

Diz *knew* that Hari was the name of the spider he had killed. It was as if he'd always known it. He nodded, unable to speak.

The spider raised the wicked-looking sword, small but as sharp as a scalpel.

Then the room went black. Diz could still see the tiny red eyes, burning in the darkness. The spider brought the sword down sharply. Again. And again. And again . . .

CHAPTER 10

FIRE

Sharon and the Rebels huddled together in the darkness, seeking the reassuring warmth of one another's bodies. The younger Rebels, in particular, were getting scared.

'Can the Howen see in the dark?' Sharon asked quietly.

'Who knows?' Moke's voice. 'Probably not. They can't see very well normally, can they? Their sense of smell will probably lead them around. Just be thankful it's not what it was when they first came. We should be safe for a while, though, depends how long the lights are out for.'

'The black-out might be only in this area,' suggested Sharon. 'At home there can be a power cut on your side of the street, but when you look out of the window, all the houses on the other side are lit up.'

'Then we'd better see just how many lights *are* out.' Els's voice.

Suddenly Sharon remembered her find. 'Of course,' she cried. 'I found some candles. Has anyone got any matches?'

'Matches?' Moke's voice. 'Candles? What are you talking about?'

Sharon explained. She handed a candle to Moke and one to Els, finding their hands in the dark. 'If we had matches we could light the candles. Then we'd be able to see.'

Then Sharon remembered that Diz had found some matches when they had first climbed into the attic. Well, one match at least. If only he were here.

'Diz has got some matches,' Sharon went on. 'I wonder . . . Do you think this might be a good time to try to rescue him? It might be easier to avoid the Howen in the dark.'

'Yes . . .' Moke's voice. 'Perhaps we should. We have to find him first, of course.'

'And find some food.' Baloney's voice.

'You're right.' Els's voice. 'Anything is better than just sitting around in the dark. Now, listen. Food team, see if you can bring back some greyroot under cover of darkness. But be careful. And the three of us will try to find Diz.'

And so the Rebels set off. But the dark was very dark, as though every molecule of air had been painted the deepest black, and it wasn't long before both groups found themselves back at the hideout, unsuccessful and unsettled. For the darkness also held the unknown: strange noises, echoes, unnamed terrors . . .

It was obvious that they could easily get separated in this dark, or just plain lost. If the Howen caught their scent they would be easily captured. And what if the lights came on when they were close to the Howen?

'Humph . . . that was a failure then.' Els's voice.

'I know what,' said Sharon, brightly. 'The Brethren have a torch.'

'They'd be no easier to reach, though, would they?'

Sharon had to admit that this was true.

The lights went out in the staffroom, but the red eyes of the spider continued to glow. Diz was trembling in fear. It was almost too much to bear, being attacked by a spider in the dark.

Diz could feel the sword hitting his wrist, but there was no pain. His arm and hand were so numb, he simply assumed he could not feel the slashes of the spider's weapon. He was glad of the dark then, because he wouldn't be able to see the blood. Then he felt pins and needles in his fingers. Feeling was returning; in fact, he could move his hand. But there was no pain.

His first reaction was to fling the great spider off, away from him. But with a massive effort of will he restrained himself. The spider had cut his bonds.

Diz felt the spider jump from his arm and land on his lap. He watched the glowing red eyes as it crossed his body to his other arm, where it hacked through the ropes binding that wrist to the chair. Carefully, Diz stretched his arms and flexed his muscles. The pins and needles gave way to a warm ache.

'Thank you,' Diz said. Then he remembered killing the other spider, Hari. 'Why did you free me?'

Because you were trapped. Because you have a great part to play in releasing the Children. And the Brethren. And the Howen. Both we and the Brethren, in our ways, know this.

'And the Howen don't?' Diz watched the red eyes

carefully. He still felt afraid of the spider, with its long, hairy legs which he couldn't see. But he held this fear in control, as if it were caught in a box, straining to get out, and he was holding the lid down tight.

The Howen are a warlike race. They are cunning and devious in the ways of battle, but they are not very intelligent. They would kill you and the Rebels, and thus seal their fate inside this rotting prison for ever. But the web has been spun. Come, I will guide you through the dark. I shall sit on your shoulder. Where do you want to go?

'I must find Sharon, my sister. She's probably with the Rebels . . . if the Howen haven't got her. What's your name?'

Hari.

Confusing, Diz thought. Two spiders, both called Hari. He felt his new friend climb his body and sit on his shoulder. Even though he knew it would do him no harm, he couldn't help the shiver that ran up his spine when he felt a leg brush against his cheek.

'I thought you were going to kill me,' Diz said, quietly.

Why would I do that?

'Because I killed Hari.'

Are you suggesting that your killing Hari could be a reason for my killing you?

'Yes.' Diz thought this was obvious, but the spider was clearly thinking it over.

What would be the sense in that?

'To get your own back. Revenge.'

Revenge . . .

It was at this moment that Diz realized the spider was talking to him in his head, not out loud at all.

Telepathy, something he didn't think ever happened. But it did. It was happening to him.

Revenge . . . a strange word. Would killing you bring Hari back to life?

'No, but . . .' Diz wasn't sure how to answer this.

Come, we must go. We Hari are creatures of the night. I am able to guide you through the darkness. The door is in front of you, a little to the left.

All the rooms were pitch black. Diz followed the spider's directions carefully. Feeling his way along passage walls wasn't too bad, but crossing empty spaces was more worrying. Every second he thought he might bump into something. This must be how a blind person feels, Diz thought, always walking forward without knowing what lies ahead, but trusting a guide dog. And here I am putting my trust in a giant spider, perched on my shoulder like a parrot.

It seemed that the longer he was in this weird building, the stranger it became. Instead of the pieces fitting together as he discovered more about it, everything was becoming more puzzling, like a dream turning into a nightmare.

Hari and Diz heard noises every now and then . . . children crying and dogs whimpering or talking in raspy whispers.

Don't worry. The voice in Diz's head was reassuring. *The Howen can smell you, but they won't do anything. They're scared of the dark.*

Diz lost track of time as they threaded their way through the dark rooms. The journey might have taken ten minutes, or it might have been an hour, before Diz heard a wonderfully familiar voice.

'Sharon!' he yelled.

'Dizzy! Is that you?' her excited voice cried back.

He made his way forward, towards the safety of his sister's voice, not noticing as the weight of the spider left his shoulder.

He felt Sharon in front of him and they threw their arms around one another and squeezed. There was one thing at least they could both be sure of in this strange, frightening world. Each other. They were real. They were from the real world and they had one another to prove it. As long as they were safe, and together, they would find a way out of this prison. Somehow they would find their way back home. Diz started laughing and Sharon did too. Then the others joined in, although what they were all laughing about none of them knew.

Diz told Sharon and the Rebels how he had managed to find them, pausing slightly before revealing how Ginger had met his end. He guessed correctly that this news would be greeted by the Rebels with mixed feelings. Ginger had turned against them, but he had once been their friend. They wouldn't have wanted him to die.

Ginger's fate wasn't fair. Nothing was fair. The Rebels were angry and upset. They were interested to hear about Hari, though. And surprised to learn that Diz had killed a spider.

'We've all seen the spiders at one time or another,' Moke said. 'They've never hurt us.'

Spiders obviously didn't have the creepy-crawly effect on the Children that they had on people like Diz.

'I didn't know the spiders could talk,' added Moke. 'They could help us in the dark, then?'

'That's good. But where is your Hari friend, Diz?' asked Els.

Looking around the room they could see no tell-tale eyes, glowing in the darkness. Diz called Hari's name, but the spider didn't appear.

Sharon suddenly remembered. 'Have you got the matches, Diz? I found a whole stack of candles.' In the excitement of finding her brother she'd forgotten to ask this before. 'Come on, the ones you found in the attic. Then we can have light.'

'There was only one live one, and anyway, I haven't got them,' Diz said glumly. 'Don't you remember? I dropped them when I came down through the trap-door. That boy picked them up when the Howen came in.'

'What boy?' Moke asked.

'Oh . . .' Diz murmured. The name had gone out of his head. What was it?

'I remember,' Sharon said. 'It was Jaro. We could look for him,' she suggested. 'If we could light some candles we'd be able to see what we were doing. This dark is creepy. And it's getting colder, too. Have you noticed?'

Now Sharon had mentioned it they could all feel the chill.

'The heating must have broken down,' Sharon went on. 'The candles might give us a little warmth.'

Els thought for a moment. 'Well, if this Jaro is in the hall we'll have no chance. But if he was in the canteen when the lights went out, or the dormitory, or somewhere between the two, and if he's stayed put, there might be a chance that we could reach him. But there's no point. The Howen would smell us.'

'Doubtful,' Moke said. 'They might smell Diz or Sharon, though.'

'No,' Diz said. 'Hari told me. They're cowards, afraid of the dark. We came through easily. And we were close to the Howen at times.'

The Rebels were undecided. But anything was better than just sitting around in the dark, waiting for nothing and feeling hungrier by the minute. So Els, Moke, Crab and Baloney, who thought they might come across some greyroot, set off with Diz and Sharon in search of Jaro.

They moved more slowly than Diz had done when he'd escaped from the staffroom. They had no spider to guide them. At every junction they had to stop and check their memories of the building. When they heard the Howen near by, they had to veer off their path. And all the time the darkness settled around them like a heavy blanket, hiding the unexpected. But after what seemed like an eternity of creeping, they had a stroke of luck.

When the lights went out, Jaro and Bel were still in the dormitory. They sat and waited in the darkness, expecting the lights to come back on at any moment. Patiently they sat huddled together, for what seemed like ages. But still no light.

'Shall we do it?' Jaro whispered, feeling for Bel's hand in the blackness.

Bel understood what he meant straight away.

'Suppose the lights come on?' she said. And then answered herself. 'So what. We might never get a chance like this again. Keep hold of me, Jaro, we'll try to find the Rebels.'

So Bel made the decision to go.

Bel and Jaro had been about to make their way back to the hall from the dormitory when the power had failed. If they'd been in the hall, where they should have been, waiting for the day's paper to arrive, they'd have been trapped. But now, the unexpected darkness was to be their friend.

They inched along corridor after corridor, not knowing where they were going, hoping they were moving away from the Howen. But as they rounded a corner, they both stiffened in fright. Whispers, scrabblings, movement. Then bump. Jaro cried out in alarm.

'Don't be scared,' Moke told the body he'd bumped into, sure that it was one of the Children. If he'd been one of them when the lights went out, he too would have tried to escape.

'What is it?' called Els from behind. 'Who is it?'

'You're the Rebels, aren't you?' Bel said. 'I'm Bel and this is Jaro. We've escaped. We want to join you.'

Jaro and Bel were astounded to learn that the Rebels had been looking for them all the while they were searching for the Rebels. But they were disappointed that they couldn't give Diz and Sharon what they wanted. Jaro no longer had the matches. They'd disappeared.

After a long discussion in the dark, conducted entirely in whispers – they were now in the main part of the building – the Rebels decided to contact the Brethren. The Brethren had a torch. They might also know why the lights had gone out. And, Baloney reminded them, the Brethren might even give them something to eat. They had done in the old days.

Diz and Sharon held hands, following the Rebels blindly through the maze of twisting passages, feeling hopelessly lost. Checking each corner and creeping across open spaces, waiting for a wall to suddenly meet them head on. All the while the noises of the Howen echoed distantly around them.

At last they entered a room, and Moke called a halt.

'Somewhere above us should be a trapdoor,' he whispered. 'How we'll get up to it, I don't know. But it's the way we'll find the Brethren.'

While the others were discussing this problem, Diz had a brainwave. He'd been pondering the loss of the matchbox from the dormitory. It must either have been found by the Brethren, which was unlikely, or by one of the Children, or by the Howen. Jaro had told him that he and Bel were among the last to leave for breakfast, so it was unlikely that one of the Children had it. It must have been the Howen. If so, what would they have done with it? Would they have known what a matchbox was? Probably not; the Children didn't. Would the Howen have thrown it away? Or would they have thought it unusual enough to keep? And if so, where would they keep it? It was just possible . . .

'Is the staffroom near here?' Diz asked.

'What's the staffroom?'

'It's a room with a pile of mouldy armchairs in the

corner. The Howen tied me up in there. And it has a door leading to the waste-disposal chute. It's where Ginger . . .'

'Oh, that room. Yes, we're very close, actually,' Moke said.

'Could you take me there?' asked Diz.

'I suppose so.' Moke sounded uncertain.

'It's important.'

'Wait for us,' Sharon said. 'Let's see the Brethren first. Anyway, I don't want us to get split up again.'

'It won't take long. Honest. Give us a couple of candles.'

'I've got one already,' Moke said.

'Then give me one,' said Diz.

'This is how we got split up before,' Sharon said, annoyed.

'Don't worry. We'll be OK.'

'I'd rather you didn't.'

'I said we'll be OK,' Diz insisted.

Diz and Moke, with a candle each and with Moke leading the way, found the staffroom without much bother.

'I think this is it,' Moke said.

Diz agreed. 'Smells like it.' He felt his way along the wall to where the shelf should be. The shelf he'd sat staring at with his hands tied to the chair. Yes, it was there. They were in the right room, sure enough. He felt his way through all the things on the shelf. The water pistol; not much good against the Howen. One trainer, a pair of shorts, a chipped mug. But no matchbox. It had to be here. This was surely the building's lost-property office. Or at least where the

Howen put the things that they took from the Children, things they had no use for.

Diz was about to give up when his fingers brushed against something small, made of rough wood. His hand closed around it. He'd found the matchbox.

'It's here,' he whispered, feeling pleased with himself.

He felt through the box for the one live match he knew should be there. It was. Good. He would have to be careful and light the candle first time. If the match went out . . .

He felt his way to the chair and carefully balanced the candle on it, leaving two hands free. The match flared like a small sun, a blinding light. Its after-image danced around the room in front of Diz's eyes. He lit the candle first time. Then he used the match to light the second candle, which he handed back to Moke.

The candle flames flickered and suddenly illuminated the room's other door. Diz crossed the room and Moke followed, holding his candle at arm's length. He had never seen a lighted candle before and it looked rather dangerous. 'Where are you going? Shouldn't we get back?'

'Have you ever been through here?' Diz asked.

Moke shook his head. 'Some of the children have. They take the paper down there. You can get to it from the cellars as well.'

'Let's go down. I'm curious to see what the waste-disposal chute looks like. It won't take a minute.'

At that moment they heard a noise from the chair. The candle had fallen on its side. Diz was about to rush over to it when he noticed the spider – rolling the candle across the seat. It reached the edge and fell to the floor.

Diz and Moke made no move. They just watched open-mouthed as another spider steered the burning candle across the floor and with a final push, rolled it into the pile of armchairs. The mouldy stuffing burst into flames. The spider scuttled away.

'Quick!' yelled Diz. 'We must put it out.'

But it was too late. The armchairs were burning fiercely and the flames had already reached the ceiling. Within seconds they licked along the wall's wooden panelling and wrapped themselves around the door.

'We'll never get through that! We'll be burned alive,' Moke cried.

'There's only one thing for it, then,' said Diz. And with trembling hands he opened the door behind him. Steps led down. Holding the remaining candle in front of them, Diz and Moke descended.

The Rebels had to admit defeat. They were no closer to getting through the trapdoor to the Brethren. Their attempt at forming a human pyramid had failed. None of them had realized how difficult it was to keep their balance in the dark.

The door to the room slammed and they spun round to face the darkness. A voice spoke to them. An icy voice that made Sharon's nerves tingle. A voice she would never forget. The voice of Feer.

'Yes, brave children. Brave, *foolhardy* children. Most of my pack are cowards, afraid of the dark. Soft whimpering curs. But some of us are made of sterner stuff. It was easy to follow your scents, especially that of the strange girl child, different from that of you so-called Rebels. Now there will be no more of your rebellious ways.'

The stink cloyed in Sharon's nostrils and she felt the Howen's body heat as they moved in. Suddenly, out of the darkness, steely claws grabbed her arm and held her in a vice-like grip.

CHAPTER 11

THE CHUTE

Moke and Diz clattered down the steps that led to the waste-disposal chute, holding the candle before them. Its flame fluttered and stuttered in the cold up-draught of air. Their footsteps echoed round the stairway.

'We've done it now,' Diz panted. 'The whole place will go up.'

'We might escape, though,' Moke called over his shoulder. 'If the building burns down we might be able to get out.'

'How?'

'Through the outside walls.'

'But where are they?'

'Well . . . I don't really know. At the Edge, I suppose.'

They reached a landing at the bottom of the staircase. More steps led down. Moke held the candle up as the boys recovered their breath.

'Have you noticed anything?' Diz asked. 'The steps are metal, more like an iron staircase. The walls are metal, too.'

A thin film of hair coated the steps; a reminder of the Howen's presence.

'We didn't start that fire, you know,' Diz went on. 'It was the spiders, although I can't think why they did it.'

'Maybe they're as crazy as the Howen.'

Diz didn't think so.

There was a door on this landing. Diz opened it. Another corridor stretching into darkness. 'This must lead to the cellars. Well, shall we go further down?'

The two boys hesitated. Having got used to the three levels of the building, Diz thought there was definitely something scary about going any lower. What horrors might be stirring in the depths? Yet Diz had already faced the stuff of his nightmares – the spiders. Why was he so scared of them, he wondered. He must have been frightened by a spider when he was a little boy, before he knew whether or not they would hurt him. But spiders were harmless, in Britain at least.

Well, however many spiders there might be lurking down those steps, or whatever else he might meet, Diz was not turning back.

'Come on,' he whispered. He took the lead and they continued down the metal staircase.

Sharon felt sick and miserable. Captured by the Howen! She wished it were all a dream. Surely there could be nothing worse than being slung across the shoulders of a huge dog-like creature, in pitch darkness, as though she were a sack of potatoes.

Earlier Feer had called this creature by name –

Brute – and he was a brute. He was certainly not handling her gently. She was only thankful she couldn't see him; just smelling him was bad enough. She could sense the other Howen with their captives beside her, all moving quickly and quietly through the blackness.

Els had called to her once, but she had been silenced by a rough voice and a slap, which Sharon had almost felt. Els's cry of pain still rang in her ears.

Els was angry. Angry that the Rebels had been captured so easily. Diz had said they could avoid the Howen. But they couldn't. The risk had been too great. She shouldn't have listened. After all, what did he know? He'd only been here one day and he'd got himself caught almost immediately. She'd been here years, surviving, getting through one day to the next. Would she grow to be a woman here, she wondered. By then the Howen would be old and feeble; men and women would take over. Would they escape? Would the greyroot last that long?

Els immediately felt guilty about being angry with Diz. It wasn't his fault, he was a stranger here. She wondered how it would all end. What was the point of it all, anyway?

Baloney felt miserable; the bumpy ride was making his rumbling stomach worse. He didn't ask much out of life, just something to eat. It was so long since he had tasted real food he had forgotten what it was like. But he clung to the notion that it must be the most wonderful thing in the world and one day, one distant day, he would taste it.

Both Jaro and Bel were already resigned to being

caught. No doubt they would simply be thrown back in with the other Children; at the worst they could expect a beating. But they both felt cheated. Their taste of freedom had been short and sour. Jaro had been talking about joining the Rebels for so long, now he'd actually done it and straight away he'd been caught. It just didn't seem fair.

Jaro thought of his mother. Was she really like the woman in his dreams? He couldn't remember. Had he conjured up her picture from some memory of the distant past? Or was she simply a figment of his imagination? Made up? He would probably never know.

In the attic, Bartholomew was tightening his belt another notch when his delicate nostrils sensed the smoke.

Food had been scarce lately. More greyroot was being eaten than was growing again and new patches were becoming harder to find. In the early days there had been an ample supply. Then, Bartholomew had been a young, fat mouse.

The others were already at their meditations – seeking out the well of peace that could be found deep in their minds. They would sit quietly and let their bodies go, tensing each set of muscles in turn and then relaxing it. Then they would softly sing the beautiful chant that led their thoughts to the well. They would look into the water of the well and see their true reflections.

The smell of smoke. It was there. Carried by the tiny motes of dust and moisture that swirled around the building on invisible currents of air. Bartholomew concentrated. He had to be sure. His whiskers twitched. Yes – it was definitely smoke.

He smiled. At last. The prophecy. Their destiny was near. He hurried to tell the others.

Moke now followed Diz as they made their way cautiously down the steps. Somewhere ahead of them was the waste-disposal chute. Moke held the candle high. The air was getting colder. They both began to shiver. The steps were still covered in hair and also with scraps of torn paper. Computer print-out, Diz realized.

Eagerly he picked some up and tried to read it. It made no sense to him, but although there were many symbols he didn't recognize, some of the letters and figures were written in the English alphabet. That was something. At least it would give him a chance when he finally got to the computer. If he ever got to it.

At last they reached the bottom. The stairway opened into a small room, again made entirely of metal. There was nothing here that reminded Diz of a school. There was a door opposite but in the centre of the floor was a hatch, as wide across as Diz was tall. It had a heavy, round cover with two silver handles.

'This is like a submarine,' he whispered.

'A submarine?'

'Yes. It's a kind of big ship that travels underwater.'

Moke looked at him blankly. 'What's a ship?'

'Never mind,' Diz sighed.

The boys stood and studied the hatch.

Moke was now so cold that the candle was trembling in his hand. 'There it is,' he said. 'The waste-disposal chute.'

Diz grabbed the hatch handles and gave a huge pull. He nearly lost his balance and fell backwards because the hatch opened easily, sliding to one side, smoothly and silently.

A stink rose to meet them. The stink of decay. They peered into the hole and darkness peered back. Moke held the candle over the edge. It was too deep to see the bottom, but the chute appeared to be some great, empty cavern. The smell reminded Diz of visits to the rubbish dump with his father. But the smell was much stronger here. If Ginger had been thrown down there he'd be dead by now, Diz thought sombrely.

Then they heard the sounds: rustling sounds, echoing from the depths below. Something, or some things, were moving about down there. Diz fancied he saw a flash of white. Were his senses playing tricks or could he see hundreds of pale, luminous eyes, shining in the darkness? No, they weren't eyes; he could see them clearly now. They were slugs. Huge white slugs.

Both boys moved back from the edge of the hole and Diz hastily swung the hatch shut. But the noises continued; scrabbling noises. The sound was behind them. They spun round. There was nothing there.

Something was banging on the other side of the unopened door. They could hear a voice, too, moaning.

Ginger!

The door opened into a large cupboard. Ginger was lying on the floor, tied up. His skin was white, almost blue, and he seemed barely conscious. Diz felt his cheek. It was as cold as marble.

*

From all over the building the spiders were gathering. From the Edge, where rooms and passageways were too narrow for children, dogs or mice to travel; from the dark corners of the attic; from the lonely rooms in the cellars, where children or animals seldom went. They crawled along rafters, through tunnels no wider than a human wrist, from beneath floorboards and from behind cupboards.

They carried with them a great and precious secret, handed down through generations of Hari – originally from the first, lost generation, from those spiders who had been trapped in a much larger web. They carried with them knowledge of their part in the prophecy: The Unwinding of the Web.

The call had gone out, passed from Hari to Hari, along a network of almost invisible silver threads. The time is near, the message said.

Sharon had only been slung over the Howen's shoulder for a few minutes, travelling through the darkness, but it seemed much longer. Now they had reached a workshop of some kind, and there was light. It was only the building's normal dim light but it seemed much brighter after the total darkness of before.

Sharon was thrown roughly to the floor, along with the other Rebel captives. She saw Brute then, her captor, and shuddered. An Alsatian – maybe even the one she had seen that first time, so long ago, as she peered innocently down through the hole in the floor of the attic.

The room looked just like her school's DT room, with benches, odd-looking machines and cupboards.

But of course there were no outside windows and no sign of any school activity. No tools, no models on display, no half-finished cranes or drawings pinned up. Along one wall was a mass of pipes, junction boxes and fuse boxes. For some reason this room must have been wired up differently from the others and had escaped the power cut.

They had come in through what would have been the woodstore in her world. There was another door at the other end of the room, but Sharon doubted that it led outside. Feer had followed them in. The Howen, who had been lounging around before Feer entered, jumped to their feet and crowded round the prisoners. Feer towered over them. This may look like the DT room, Sharon thought, but I bet we're not about to be told how to use a saw correctly.

Fear spoke. His voice was quiet, almost matter-of-fact, but it had a nasty, unsettling edge to it. Suddenly a thought came into Sharon's head. He's mad. More than just a mean, vicious dog, but mad, too. She thought of the rabies signs she'd seen at the docks, and the terrifying stories she had heard. She shuddered.

Feer spoke directly to Sharon. 'I have had enough of this nonsense. What is your name?'

'Sharon Gillespie.' She took a deep breath, told herself to be calm, not to be panicked by this mad and monstrous dog. It was the first time she had actually seen one of the Howen close to. She felt like throwing up.

'Sharon . . . of course. Well, Sharon, I think you can help us . . . and I think we can help you. You and that boy know the way out of this building. He is a fool. He wouldn't tell us. But you are not a fool.' He paused. 'Are you a fool, Sharon?'

She shook her head. What was this leading up to?

His voice took on an icy sweetness. 'Only a fool would like to see her friends hurt, wouldn't she? Would you like to see your friends hurt?'

She shook her head again. So that was it. She glanced round at the others. At Els, Baloney, Jaro and Bel. They were following the conversation closely, their faces white. Feer was watching her. She would have to think of something. Something convincing, and quick. Diz had always said she was the clever one . . .

'Come along,' Feer snarled. 'None of us want to see your friends hurt, so tell us what we want to know. Tell us how to get out of this accursed place. Must we hurt your friends, eh?' He was becoming agitated, angry.

The other Howen were stirring.

'All right,' Sharon said, fighting to keep her voice calm, under control. 'I'll tell you all I know.'

'That's better,' Feer said, his voice again sickly soft.

'Well . . . we came here through the attic. But we don't know how we got here, we really don't. If we knew the way back we'd have gone by now.'

'But that's what you were doing when we caught you.' Feer snarled. 'On your way out of here through the attic.' He leant forward. 'You'll have to do better than that.' Feer raised his paw, as though about to give a signal.

'Wait! I do know how we can escape. All of us.'

'Go on.'

'The computer. That's where the answer is. The Big Cheese, the Brethren call it. Where you get all the paper from. It's a computer, a kind of machine.'

'Yes, yes. But we have searched the paper. Every day we search the paper. It tells us nothing.'

'But it's a computer. I've worked with them before and Diz knows even more about them than I do. If we could get into its programs –'

'Enough!' Feer barked. 'You cannot get *into* it. Only the gods can do that. You lie. Now – how did you get here? Tell us the way out or you will all perish!' He was shouting now, showering Sharon and the others with slobber.

But even while they were talking, Sharon had become aware of a subtle change in the atmosphere. A different smell, lying behind the nauseous smell of the Howen. The smell of smoke. Something was burning.

Just as it looked as if Feer was about to lash out, Raffer burst into the room. His red eyes were wide with panic, and he seemed hysterical.

'Fire! Fire! There is a great fire! The building is burning. We will all be killed. Run, flee. Fire!'

Through the open door, a thin ball of smoke rolled over Raffer's head from the darkness behind him, uncurled lazily and began to fill the room.

Feer watched the smoke for a few seconds. 'Why, that's perfect,' he said. Then he regarded Sharon and the Rebels with a stare full of hate. 'Tie them up,' he barked. 'We'll give them to the fire.'

CHAPTER 12

SMOKE

The central rooms of the building were thick with choking black smoke. The sort of smoke that causes most deaths in a house fire. It spreads quickly and it suffocates. There's never time to go back into a building, however far away the flames might seem, because the deadly, choking smoke will be there, waiting. So it was that the Howen, the Children, the Rebels, the Brethren, the Hari, Sharon, and all the other creatures who had become trapped in the building knew about the fire before they had actually seen the blaze or heard the crackle of flames.

The smoke was everywhere, but it couldn't be seen in the darkness. It was like a black fog in the night. It rolled along passageways, crawled under doors and filled rooms. Here comes my master, it seemed to say. My master – Death.

The Howen had been brave warriors in days gone by, a noble race. But they had listened too long and too often to their cruel captains and greedy generals. Centuries of war had made them what they now were – callous, mean and vindictive. They were also terrified of fire.

As the smoke spread through the darkness, so did the howls of the Howen. Many of them panicked, running blindly, colliding with walls, crashing through doors. The building was full of their cries. Help! Help! Run! Flee!

A few of the Howen, however, kept their heads and tried to make some sense of the bedlam. They could be heard calling through the darkness. 'Keep calm. Find the stairs. Go down to the cellars.' But all the time other Howen were careering this way and that, causing chaos, as though their brains were no longer anything to do with their bodies.

Feer retained control throughout. His presence was such that he calmed the Howen in the workshop, whose first instinct had been to panic. He also calmed Raffer, who had run petrified into the room to warn his master.

Feer ordered the Howen to tie up Sharon and the Rebels. The dogs bound the children's hands and feet and then looped the ropes under the heavy bench legs. But all the time the Howen kept glancing around nervously as more smoke drifted into the room.

'When the fire has burnt itself out,' Feer said, a horrid smile on his face, 'we will emerge from the cellars and escape. We'll be safe down there, where the stone won't burn. The fire will surely burn the building down and then we'll be free. If it doesn't, we'll go up into the attic. If that really is the way you came in, girl, we'll find the way out.'

He motioned the Howen to leave and followed them, pausing in the doorway to look back at the frightened Rebels.

'You, of course, will not be there when we escape. You will have been burnt alive and charred to a cinder.' They heard the echoes of Feer's evil laugh as the Howen disappeared into the smoke and the darkness.

The Rebels lay in the empty room, tied to the benches and scared. No one spoke as they watched the smoke begin to fill the room. They started coughing.

The Children sat in the hall in darkness. None cried. They just accepted the black-out and simply sat. At first some talked in hushed whispers, but they soon ran out of things to say. Others went to sleep.

Although the darkness had frightened many of the Howen, the chief guards were not upset by it. They still took pride in the Howen tradition and were not prepared to let something as trivial as a black-out distract them from their duty. They stood in the hall with the Children, and waited.

After a long time, Raffer appeared to tell them that one of the rooms had light and that they should go there. Being good guard dogs they locked the hall door behind them, making sure that the Children could not escape while they were away.

When the fire started and smoke began to seep beneath the door into the hall, the Children were still sitting or lying in the same places. The ones at the front noticed the smell first and word quickly passed around the hall. Soon they could all smell it.

A group of them gathered round the door and tried to force it open. It was no good. It opened inwards. After a few half-hearted kicks they gave up and wandered back to their places. Why bother? There was nothing to gain from leaving the hall. So what if there was a little smoke? Of course, there were so many things they could have done. But they simply sat and waited, resigned to whatever fate had in store.

Elsewhere in the building another group sat and did nothing. It took a long time for the smoke to reach Far Point, and by then it was too late for those Rebels who had stayed behind to play any part in the unfolding events. They could have gone with Sharon, Els and the others, or, knowing the Howen wouldn't attack them in the dark, they could have gone looking for food. But they, too, just sat in the darkness and waited.

In the depths of the building, in the cold, Diz and Moke looked down at Ginger, the Rebel who had tricked Sharon and betrayed the Brethren. His face looked ghostly by the candle's pale light. His eyes were closed, his breathing shallow, and his lips were no longer pink, but blue. They untied his bonds, leaving the rope behind in the cupboard.

'We'll have to move him,' Diz said. 'Get him somewhere warm and get his circulation going.'

Diz showed Moke how to stick the candle carefully to the floor and then the two of them sat Ginger up. Diz took his school blazer off and helped Ginger's awkward arms into the sleeves. Ginger was taller than Diz and the sleeves were a little short, but the jacket wasn't too tight.

'It doesn't suit him,' Diz joked.

'Come on, Ginger,' Moke said. 'Come on. We can't

carry you up all those stairs. You'll have to try to walk.'

Ginger opened his eyes and smiled weakly. 'I'm . . . all . . . right,' he whispered. It was plain he wasn't.

'It's OK,' Moke reassured him. 'Come on, now. Try to stand up.'

Together the boys managed to coax Ginger to his feet, their arms round his shoulders. They supported him as best they could, considering his height, and considering they had somehow to hold the candle. They started to climb the stairs. Suddenly Ginger began to shiver and the shiver grew until his whole body was shaking as though it were out of control. Diz and Moke hung on grimly; they were four steps up, but it seemed likely they would be back at the bottom any second. Diz thought they would drop the candle, or that it would be blown out by the sudden movements. But the shaking gradually stopped as Ginger slowly regained control of himself.

They resumed their climb and Ginger seemed to be getting stronger as they neared the top of the first flight of stairs. At last they reached the landing and sat down heavily, out of breath. Here, sitting by the door that led out to the cellars, they could smell the smoke drifting down the next flight of stairs from the staffroom above.

And here too, suspended on a silver thread, a spider was waiting for them.

The spiders started the fire, Diz thought. Perhaps this was one of the culprits. Were all the spiders in on it? He had no way of knowing. Should he trust this spider? He thought he probably shouldn't. But he would. After all, a spider had rescued him.

The Making of the Web is at hand, the spider said. *You must go to the Spinner now. Hurry.*

'What's the Spinner?' Diz asked.

The Brethren call it the Big Cheese. It is the source of all power.

'Oh yes, the computer. Do you mean the three of us must go?'

It doesn't matter who goes with you. But you, Diz, are needed there now.

Diz realized from the puzzled look on Ginger's and Moke's faces that they couldn't hear the spider's voice. They must think I'm mad, he thought, talking out loud to myself. He turned back to the Hari.

'Well, I'll have to take Moke because I don't know the way.' He turned to Ginger. 'Do you think you can make it to the computer room? You know, the room where the paper comes out?'

Ginger nodded.

'You're talking to the spider, then,' Moke said, amazed. Diz nodded.

Goodspin, the spider said and swiftly climbed his web. The meeting was obviously at an end.

'Come on, then,' Diz sighed. Would this nightmare never end?

'So where are we going?' Moke asked.

'The computer room. The Brethren call it the Big Cheese. Sharon said she'd been there. You'll have to lead the way.'

And from the darkness the spider watched as the ungainly humans struggled through the door and disappeared into the shadows.

*

But what of Crab? Little Crab, the smallest and youngest of the Rebels?

When Sharon and her friends were trying to find their way up into the attic and the Howen had surrounded them, Crab had slipped to one side, unnoticed in the darkness and confusion of bodies, noise, movement and scents. He had crept to the corner of the room and sat very still. Once, long ago, the Howen would have spotted him immediately, but time and poor food had dulled their usually keen senses. Even Feer missed Crab, so intent was he on capturing Sharon.

Crab didn't want to be left alone in the dark and so he nervously followed the Howen and their captives, keeping as close as he dared, until he saw them disappear into the lighted room. Then he opened a classroom door, closed it quietly behind him and waited inside. He had a clear view of the corridor by lifting the curtain that hung over the door's glass pane.

He waited. After a while Raffer ran by and then, quite soon, the Howen came marching back the other way, followed by Feer. Crab could only dimly see their outlines, but Feer's great bulk was unmistakable.

Feer suddenly stopped. Right outside the classroom door. Crab froze. He let the curtain fall back into place, and huddled himself up tight behind the door. In his mind he saw Feer's face, the red eyes, the long, yellow teeth and slobering jaws. An eternity passed. Then he heard the handle turn.

In the attic the Brethren were ready. Smoke was curling up from between the joists. It was acrid and overpowering to the Brethren's finely tuned sense of smell. Nevertheless, the mice seemed in high spirits. They were grouped around the Game of Changes.

'There are two possible moves,' said Reginald. 'Moving the Red Sun to the final square or moving the pawns to the final spiral.'

'It has to be the pawns,' Bartholomew said, and the other four agreed with him. They nodded, eagerly.

'I disagree,' Reginald said, and without waiting for further discussion he leant forward and pushed the Red Sun on to the centre square.

Bartholomew gasped.

From close by they heard a crash, and smoke billowed into the attic.

Crab, crouching behind the classroom door in the dark, heard the handle turn. Feer had found him. But suddenly there was a great shrieking and howling in the corridor. The doorknob slipped back into place and the Howen leader moved on down the passageway. Crab let out a long sigh of relief.

But then Crab smelled the smoke. What was it? He had never come across anything like it before. He waited a few moments more and let himself carefully into the corridor. There the smoke nearly took his breath away. With his eyes watering he ran quickly to the yellow rectangle of light ahead of him.

Sharon and the Rebels were overjoyed to see Crab. Only Els didn't seem surprised, just relieved. Sharon had forgotten all about Crab, Baloney had been more concerned about his empty stomach and Bel and Jaro had never really had a chance to register who was there and who wasn't, in the dark. But Els hadn't forgotten him. Els was the leader and Crab was in her charge. Crab was actually her favourite, though she had never let on. Maybe, if they ever escaped, she would tell him.

The ropes were tied tightly, too tightly for Crab to undo. But by heaving up the bench it was possible to slip the ropes under the legs and free the Rebels that way. It wasn't long before they were all standing, rubbing their wrists to restore their circulation.

The smoke, gathering above them, now hid the high ceiling. Their eyes were watering.

'Well done,' Els said. She wrapped her arms around Crab's frail body and gave him a big hug. He beamed with pleasure.

'We must get down to the cellars,' Sharon urged.

'No,' said Els, sharply. 'We have to get to the Children. We can't leave them up here. Do you know where they are, Bel?'

'Probably in the hall,' Bel replied.

'OK, then. Let's go.'

'Wait,' Sharon said. 'I've had an idea.' She ran over to the sink. She'd noticed a roller-towel machine attached to the wall above it. She turned on a tap and water gushed out. Good! The others watched impatiently.

'Give me a hand,' She called. 'We have to tear this towel into strips.'

The towel wouldn't tear easily, but with four children pulling in two different directions it soon ripped. Sharon wet the strips under the tap and they wound them around their noses and mouths to help protect themselves from the smoke. Then they followed Bel and Jaro out into the choking darkness.

Sharon had seen pictures of hell at Sunday school. Pictures painted by artists who must surely have visited that terrible place of smoke, flame and torture. And this must be what hell is like, she thought. She could hear the flames and feel the temperature gradually rising but she could see nothing.

She held on to Baloney in front of her and staggered on into the darkness. She felt frightened, as though she were in a black cave deep underground and the roof was about to collapse and the whole weight of the earth above was going to crush her. Every few seconds they heard a distant crash as some part of the building collapsed. All the time the smoke got thicker and the air got warmer, but still they stumbled on. Twice, a huge shape pushed past them and Sharon caught the reek of Howen. But each time the dog was too intent on saving his own skin to bother with them.

Els was at the front with Jaro and Bel. At first they roughly pieced together the route from what they knew of the building. But they were soon in territory familiar to Bel and Jaro and the pace quickened. Sharon found the wet towel helped her breath, but her eyes were continually watering. She had to keep wiping them as she staggered on.

It was really hot now. The Rebels turned a corner and saw the fire for the first time.

'What is it?' Crab cried.

'Fire,' Els said. 'It destroys everything and everyone in its path.'

Crab felt for Els's hand. 'I don't like it,' he said, but his muffled words were lost against the roar of the flames.

The far end of the corridor was ablaze, the flames creeping towards them. The hall was ahead of them. Gritting their teeth they forced themselves on and reached the hall door. It was locked.

Sharon pulled the towel from her face and started coughing. 'Are there any other doors?' she yelled, remembering the fire exits in her own school hall.

'No,' Jaro yelled back.

Sharon realized then that they were gradually moving back, being forced to retreat from the hall door by the heat of the burning walls.

'Break it down,' she yelled. 'We must get the Children out.'

But now the hall door was beyond their reach, the flames were forcing them further back, the heat was too great.

'The Children will die,' Sharon sobbed.

CHAPTER 13

THE WEB

Six excited Brethren clambered down the rope ladder into the room where Diz and Sharon had first seen the Howen. Once assembled, they walked without hesitation, despite the dark and the smoke, between the desks and out into the corridor.

They walked in single file according to age. Reginald the Abbot, the eldest, led them, while Gladly, the youngest, brought up the rear. The smoke, which had caused so many problems for Rebels, Children and Howen alike, didn't seem to bother the Brethren. They marched forwards – towards the fire.

Sharon and the Rebels were at the door to the hall, trying to shield themselves from the blistering heat. The towels over their mouths were steaming and almost dry. Sharon knew that unless they did something quickly, not only would the Children have no chance, but the Rebels too would be suffocated by the smoke. Her eyes were streaming, she felt dizzy and the smoke in her lungs was making her cough. But what could she do?

Then the Brethren arrived. They acted as though

the fire were no more than a magic-lantern show, pretty pictures projected on the walls. Ignoring the blistering heat, they walked up to the door. Sharon and the others watched wide-eyed as the mice stood, three abreast, each side of the doorway. The door itself was burning and flames began to lick around the Brethren's robes, but they didn't seem to notice this threat. Reginald gave the door a hefty kick and it fell inwards with a crash. Suddenly the Brethren raised their arms. Their flowing robes formed a shield against the fire as they stood along each side of the corridor.

By now, the Children had roused themselves. The heat and the smoke and the danger could no longer be ignored. They had begun to crowd around the door, pushing and jostling to get out, until the heat had driven them back. Even the flag across the back of the stage had started to smoulder as the heat came through the wall. Then they had crouched in the furthest corner of the hall, their eyes wide with fear and panic.

At last they saw the door crash inwards and flames lick hungrily around the frame. As the Children stared out through the flaming doorway at the two rows of Brethren, their robes lit up by the fire, they seemed to be looking down an avenue of shining gold that led towards a tunnel of deep, cool black. And they heard Reginald's voice, as though someone were talking to them from the edge of a dream. He was urging them calmly through, but telling them to hurry.

Now, as if their fear and panic had been magically lifted, the Children filed quickly and quietly through the burning door, shielded from the hungry flames by the Brethren and their robes.

'Take them to the room with the light,' Reginald ordered the Rebels as the Children filed past. 'There's another door there. It leads down to safety. Children, this is your chance to defeat the Howen. Take it!'

Els took command. 'Hold on to the person in front,' she yelled over the crackling noise of the blaze. 'Now follow me.'

And so she led the great crocodile of Children away from the fierce red and black kaleidoscope of flame and smoke, back along the corridor to the workshop.

Sharon watched in fascination as the last of the Children came through, and with horror − as the robes of the Brethren began to smoulder. The last child, a young boy called Armen, passed through and the Brethren lowered their arms. Reginald looked directly at Sharon.

'Don't worry,' he said in a pure, clear voice which cut through the roar of the fire. 'Organize the Children. This will be your only chance. Take it!' Then, seeing Sharon's alarm, 'Don't worry about us. It is our destiny. Go on. Hurry!'

To Sharon's amazement Reginald and his followers then turned towards the heart of the fire. They walked away from her, towards the furnace. Sharon stared in disbelief. There were tears in her eyes, and not only from the smoke, as the Brethren walked into the flames. Then the spell seemed to break. She was about to follow the others when she saw Reginald's red hanky on the ground. She picked it up, unable to hold the tears back any longer. She ran blindly back towards the workshop, grieving and confused.

*

Diz, Moke and Ginger had made their way through the underground passages to the computer room without incident. Ginger was just about able to walk on his own, as his body regained some of the heat it had lost and his circulation returned to normal. Diz and Moke had tried talking to him, but he only grunted.

The office hallway was so brightly lit it hurt their eyes. Just as well the lights work here, Diz thought; the candle had burned down to a stub. Both Diz and Moke, who had taken turns holding it, had small burns on their hands from the candle wax, which was also splattered over their clothes.

'There must be a separate source of power here,' Diz said as Moke opened the door to the computer room and they walked hesitantly in.

'Wow!' Diz gasped. 'That is some weird machine.'

Looking at the computer in the pale-blue light of the room, Diz thought the answers to all their problems could finally be solved. But would he be able to operate such a complex machine? While Moke watched, Ginger slumped by the door and shivered.

It was certainly a large computer. The blip moved across the huge, triangular screen, just as Sharon had described it. Diz looked at the keys. Some had recognizable letters on them. He reached forward and lightly tapped a key, the letter D for Diz.

'Ouch!'

He drew his hand away sharply. Yes, an electric shock. Not a bad one, though. He had, after all, been half-expecting it.

'Are you all right?' Moke asked.

He nodded. He tried one of the bigger keys.

A shock.

He tried what he guessed was the space bar.

Another shock.

No effect on the screen at all.

Although the shocks weren't very strong, they were still painful and Diz thought three were enough. He couldn't really bring himself to touch the keyboard again. There had to be something else. He looked around the wall, around the screen, searching for an on/off switch, for a clue – but to what he didn't know. Yet there had to be something. Some way to make the computer work.

Then he spotted it. It was obvious, really. Set in the centre of a blue triangle was a triangular hole, located to the right of the central pad of keys. A keyhole? A key of some kind was obviously needed to activate the computer. A triangular key. But where could it be?

Diz sighed. He should have known things wouldn't be that easy. A key! It could be anywhere. How on earth would they find it?

A key . . . Something nagged him; half a memory, lying just out of his mind's reach. He explained the problem to Moke and Ginger. 'We have to find the key. It fits in here.' He showed them the triangular hole. 'Search this room and the hall outside. It must be here somewhere.'

Moke began to search. Ginger sat down again. Diz stared at the monitor – at the tiny blip which blinked across the screen every couple of seconds. He knew he had the answer. But what was it? The clue was somewhere in the building, he'd seen it. But where?

*

The rescued Children and the Rebels began to file into the workshop, now full of smoke. The ceiling could no longer be seen for the black fog above their heads. The far door, the door that Reginald had told them led to the safety of the cellars, was locked. Els and Jaro kicked, shook and rattled it – but it wouldn't open. And as they struggled with the door the room filled with Children, faces blackened by soot, throats sore and lungs aching from the smoke.

'It won't shift. It won't shift,' Jaro wailed, thumping the door violently.

'That's not the way,' Els said, trying to calm him. 'Losing our tempers won't help.'

Sharon arrived. 'We need something to batter it down,' she suggested.

They looked around.

'The bench,' said Els.

The Rebels and some of the Children gathered round the heavy bench. On a count of three they lifted it and swung it as hard as they could into the door. There was a great crash of splintering wood, the door caved in and the lock went clattering into the darkness. Cool air blew into their faces.

Steps led down. They descended into the refreshing, damp air of the cellars. In the dark, Els led the way along a long winding corridor which eventually led to a large arched area from which tunnels seemed to branch out. There was no sign of the Howen. A dim light shone from beyond one of the arches. From the size of the place Sharon reckoned they must be directly beneath the hall.

Gradually the room was filled with the Children.

Els made them all sit around her on the floor in a half circle. She could just make out their faces in the half-light. As the last of the Children arrived, Els called the Rebels to one side and outlined her plan. It meant they would have to go back up to the burning building. Although reluctant at first, in the end they agreed.

Only Jaro spoke out directly against the plan. He had finally found the courage to escape, been almost immediately caught, and had escaped again. The excitement was too much for him. All he wanted to do now was sit with the Children and take no further part. Bel held his hand and quietly explained.

'Sometimes you have to make a really big effort to get what you want, even if the effort seems more than you can manage. You have to do that little bit more. Do you want to be trapped here for ever?' Jaro shook his head. 'This could be our chance to escape. I mean *really* escape. A chance to go home. Home to your mum. You want that, don't you?' Jaro nodded. 'Come on, then. We have to try.'

Jaro knew she was right. He had to try. Still holding hands, Jaro and Bel followed the Rebels back up the steps.

Sharon stayed with Els. A warning from her past came to mind as she watched the Rebels leave. Never go back into a burning building.

At last the Children settled down. The coughing stopped and so did the excited whispering. Els spoke. She knew what she wanted to say, but she wasn't sure how to say it. At last, here was their big chance to defeat the Howen, to be free. But she would have to convince the Children that they could beat the Howen and that would be hard. After all, many of the Children had known no other life.

'We'll wait here for the fire to die down then, shall we?' she asked. She noticed one or two heads nodding in the gloom. No one spoke. 'We'll be OK if we wait here, I expect. The walls down here won't burn. We'll be safe enough.' She paused. Again one or two Children nodded but there was little general response.

'Then, when the fire's gone out, you can all go back upstairs,' she went on. 'Back to the Howen. I'm sure they'll be pleased to see you all. I expect you'll want to see them, too, eh?' Still hardly any reaction, although Sharon fancied some of the Children shifted uncomfortably.

She raised her voice a little. 'Who wants to go back to the Howen, then? Who wants the Howen telling them what to do every day? "Time to get up. Time to eat. Time to work. Sort the paper out. Time to sleep." Who wants that?' Still no one spoke. 'Who wants to be a prisoner for the rest of their lives? Who wants to be at the Howen's beck and call, be one of the Howen's pets on a lead? Do any of you want that? Really?' Armen, sitting at the front, shook his head. There were murmurs from the back.

'None of you,' Els said quietly. 'None of you want it. Of course you don't. Well, you don't *have* to be prisoners.'

'Yes we do,' a boy's voice said, heavy with despair.

'I am not the Howen's prisoner,' Els said angrily. 'I don't do what they say. Look – for the first time we can defeat them. We can beat them. Don't you see?

132

They're afraid of the dark and they're terrified of the fire. You saw them panicking. You saw them running about screaming.'

Now she could see the idea catching on. But the Children still needed a push. 'The Howen are scared. They're scared of the dark and they're scared of the fire but we're not. We can use that. Don't you see? They'll be scared of *you*!'

At that moment, right on cue, the other Rebels came running into the room wielding spluttering fire-brands. They had made torches from broken furniture and they held them high, lighting the room with a flickering red glow. The Children stared.

Armen jumped to his feet and cheered, waving his fist in the air. 'Down with the Howen,' he yelled. Another boy jumped up, then a girl. Now all the Children rose to their feet, cheering, yelling, 'Down with the Howen! Down with the Howen!'

After years of oppression, domination and mistreatment, they were ready to shout for a freedom they could not even remember. They might not have known what freedom meant but they had experienced tyranny. They had spent their lives being ordered about by their cruel masters and they were ready to fight back. If freedom meant no more Howen, then they wanted it. With torches burning and a fire in their hearts, they could overturn the Howen's rule. Now was their chance and they would take it.

'We'll split into two groups,' the delighted Els shouted at the Rebels above the noise. 'Jaro and Bel, you take one group. The rest come with me and Crab. The Howen are down here somewhere – let's find

them. We'll hit them before they can work out what's
going on. Let's go!'

'Wait! Look!' Sharon shouted.

The ceiling above them was alive with the swarming
shapes of spiders.

Bull had lost Alice, his pet, in the confusion of smoke
and darkness. Now he sat quietly in a cool corner of a
dark, deserted cellar room. Feer had told the Howen
they would be safe down here. He'd had one nasty
moment, almost coming face to face with the Prowler.
But he'd squeezed himself into an alcove, heart beating
wildly, and luckily the beast had passed him by.

He hated not being able to see, but he hated the fire
more. Still, it was peaceful here, crouching on the
paved floor with his strong back against a cold stone
wall. He was beginning to doze off when he saw
something that woke him instantly. Eight tiny red
eyes. A spider. And that meant food.

He eased himself slowly forward. With luck it
wouldn't notice him in the darkness and he would
catch it. A big, fat, juicy spider. Bull's mouth was
watering at the thought. The Howen had caught hardly
any spiders in the last few months. Perhaps they had
all moved to the cellars. This one was scuttling away
from him now, and quite quickly. There might be
more of them. He would follow it. He could easily
keep up with the spider and he could pounce if it
noticed him and tried to escape. Meanwhile, he would
let it lead him to its lair. There, he felt sure, he would
find a feast of spiders.

The spider was moving quickly now. Bull followed
the eight-legged meal as it scuttled along first one

corridor, then another. He began to daydream. A feast of giant spiders or, better still, a nice leg of mouse or, better still, child ... Bull hardly noticed the noise of shouting or the smell of smoke in the air, so intent was he on following his prey, dreaming his dreams. He hardly noticed, that is, until six Children leapt out in front of him, brandishing burning torches.

Caught off-guard, he panicked and turned to flee, but three more Children were behind him, waving and screaming, 'Get the Howen! Get the Howen!'

A club caught him a heavy blow across his back. He snarled, turned instantly and brushed the stick easily aside, going for the boy holding it. Another blow caught him across the back of his legs and he nearly lost his balance, but not before his huge paw had grabbed the first boy's wrist.

Then a spider landed on his head. Another landed on his shoulder. He felt a strand of thick, sticky webbing wind around his eyes and another around his body. He let go of the boy and tried to brush the spiders off. Another blow caught him across the back. More spiders fell on him and he felt himself toppling forward.

'Stop!' Bull cried. 'Let me go. Leave me alone!' Still the blows rained down. Then the pain stopped, but the sticky strands were wound so tightly around his body that he couldn't move. He lay there, looking pathetically up at his captors through the web which covered his face, as they stared down at him, grinning broadly.

'Let's find another one,' Jaro whooped triumphantly, and with jubilant cheers the Children were off to search out more of their former masters. The spiders, too, were off – to find more Howen to lead into ambushes. They were, of course, particularly skilled in the ancient craft of setting traps.

Sharon soon found herself back in the computer room. It was very close to where Els had roused the Children beneath the hall. She'd been left there to try and help Diz while the others rushed off to hunt the Howen.

She and her brother hugged one another happily. They were together again. And now at last, at long last, she thought, a chance of freedom.

'The Children are after the Howen,' Sharon finally said. 'The spiders are helping. I don't think the Howen have got a chance. Then we can escape.' She gave Ginger an icy stare. 'No thanks to you, though.'

She told them all that had happened. Moke wanted to rush down and join in at once. 'No,' Diz said. 'We must find the key.'

Diz showed Sharon the triangular hole in the computer's keyboard. 'That's the answer,' he said. 'I'm sure of it. If we could only –'

He stopped in mid-sentence and stared at his sister.

'What's up?' she asked.

'Have they caught Feer?'

'I shouldn't think so, not yet,' Sharon replied.

'Well, we'll have to find him. I've just remembered where I saw that key. The key to the computer. It's the blue crystal hanging round Feer's neck.'

CHAPTER 14

THE KEY

Feer knew something was wrong. Something was tickling at his sixth sense, a sense extremely well developed in the higher Howen. He had become separated from his pack when he, and the few Howen he had managed to gather to him, had met the Prowler in one of the dark cellar passageways. That was the last straw for the Howen and they had scattered like woodlice from beneath an upturned stone.

Feer had been taking them to the waste-disposal chute. As far as he knew, it formed the lowest part of the building and was made of iron – which wouldn't burn. He thought the underground passages would probably be safe, but if the floors above caught fire he was afraid the whole building would collapse on their heads.

And so he made his way cautiously to the iron steps that led down. But he was not alone. In one hand he held his sword and in the other he held Alice's lead, dragging the reluctant girl along behind him. It was typical of Bull, he thought, to have lost her, but he wouldn't be so careless.

Unlike the other Howen, Feer was unafraid of the dark and his sense of direction was unerring. Yet as he padded through the underground passages with Alice in tow, he knew something was out of place. Then he realized what it was. He was being followed. Whatever it was made no sound and gave off no scent, but he knew that someone or something was watching him. He turned round quickly in mid-stride. He saw nothing – only blackness. But no, he could just make out lots of tiny red spots, glowing in the dark. Eyes. Yes, the spiders were following him.

He was not afraid of spiders either. Their toy swords could be painful, but one swipe from him and a spider was a smear of blood and fur. He turned and strode on.

At last he came to the familiar iron door. How many hours of wasted time had they spent bringing their rubbish through here? Lately, of course, they had hardly bothered. He hustled Alice through the door and slammed it shut behind them. Then he pushed the concealed button that locked the door and smiled as he heard the hidden bolt click into place. Roughly pushing Alice ahead of him, he descended through the darkness to the waste-disposal chute itself.

'Well,' Els shouted, a big grin on her face, 'it looks like we've won. We've beaten the Howen.'

A great cheer went up.

'I told you we could do it – and we did!'

They cheered once more. The Children were again gathered in the large room beneath the hall. They were excited. More excited than Els had ever seen them – and with good reason. The spiders had been relaying via Diz reports of Howen captures over the last hour and, miraculously, none of the Children had been hurt.

It had taken Els five minutes to calm them down so that she could tell them the good news and now their excitement burst out again.

'Did you see Raffer? I tripped him up.'

'Yeah, but I got his sword.'

'I fought two of them single-handed.'

'Only two?'

At last Els could be heard again. 'We've almost beaten the Howen – but there's one more thing to do. Our new friends, Sharon and Diz, will explain.'

Nervously Sharon stepped forward. Pale faces seemed to dance before her in the gloom. Spiders clung to the walls and ceiling, their eyes a myriad of tiny lights, like a city seen from a plane. Yes, the Howen were almost beaten. But one had eluded them – the most dangerous Howen of them all. Now she had to explain how important his capture was. She cleared her throat.

'The fire is still out of control above us – burning the building down. We have to stop it or the floors will burn and the whole lot will collapse on top of us,' she said.

'But what can we do?' a frightened voice piped up. 'We can't fight the fire.'

Sharon felt the Children suddenly lose heart. 'There *is* something we can do,' she said. 'We know how to work the computer; the machine that spews out the paper.' She wondered whether they would understand her. Els should have told them, she was much better at communicating. 'But we need the key –'

'The key,' interrupted Diz, 'will give us access to the computer. Then we'll be able to escape.'

There was a baffled silence.

Els spoke. 'Look. There are some things we none of us understand. You know that. Why we're all here, for instance. Do any of you remember what life was like before? When you could see the sky? When you could smell the grass? When you could hear birds singing?' Some of the older children were nodding. Jaro could see his mother, coming to him in his dreams. 'Well, it can be like that again. We've beaten the Howen, haven't we?'

There were nods and approving murmurs.

'Then listen,' Els said, her voice loud and clear. 'Freedom is within our grasp. Diz and Sharon don't come from our world. They *know* what the paper means. They can make the machine open the doors. We've rid ourselves of the Howen and now we can be free. But there's one thing we need to open the door. The door is locked – so we need the key.'

'But we haven't got it,' a girl's voice shouted from the back.

'No,' another cried. 'Where is it? How can we get it?'

'It's round Feer's neck,' Sharon said calmly. 'We have to capture Feer to get the key.'

'He can't fight us all,' Moke chipped in. 'We beat his dogs, now we'll beat him.'

'But where is he?' Armen asked. 'We've searched the whole place.'

There was silence. Then Ginger, who had taken no

part at all in the proceedings so far, spoke up. 'No, we haven't. I bet he's at the chute.'

'Of course!' Els yelled delightedly. 'That's where he'll be. The waste-disposal chute.'

But before she could say any more the Children had climbed to their feet and, like a wave, were flowing from the room and out into the passages that led to the chute. They were cheering and shouting. Another chance to act. The taste of triumph was still sweet in their mouths. So they rushed through the darkness, along the underground ways to the place they knew so well.

Els, Sharon and Diz watched them leave, and were about to follow.

Wait! They each heard the Hari speaking in their heads. *We were about to tell you where Feer was. But you won't reach him that way. The door to the chute is locked.*

The children looked at one another in dismay.

You'll have to go the other way – through the building.

'But we can't possibly,' Diz said. 'It's burning. We'll be killed.'

You must, the spiders said. *It is the only way. But it won't be so bad. You'll have help.*

'Help?' Sharon questioned. Whoever could help them?

Now hurry. You may not have much time. Go by the main staircase.

'I suppose we'd better try it,' Sharon said. Diz and Els nodded in half-hearted agreement.

There's one more thing you should know, the Hari said. *Feer holds Alice captive.*

*

Sharon, Diz and Els climbed the main staircase. The stink of burnt wood assailed their nostrils and the air grew suddenly warm. Above them all was dark. They could feel warm ashes under their feet. At the top a voice greeted them. It was a male voice that, at first, none of the children recognized, although it stirred something in Sharon's memory. 'Follow me,' it said.

'Wait!' Sharon exclaimed. She had just remembered something. All this time spent wandering around in the darkness and she had a pocketful of candles. What a dumbo! But there was no means of lighting them here; the fire seemed to have burnt itself out, in this part of the building at least. 'It's OK,' she said.

'Hold my gown and follow,' the voice said.

She held tightly to the great bulky figure that loomed before her and felt Diz clinging to her. No doubt Els was holding on to him at the back. They set off at a brisk pace, blindly following their leader.

As they passed a burning wall Sharon lit one of her candles. The ceilings and walls looked as though they'd been painted with soot. Her feet felt warm as she walked over hot ash. Sharon couldn't see much of the shadowy figure she was following. She knew only that his robe was of a coarse, dark material. The creature had a pole or staff of some kind which he occasionally used to push aside an obstacle or tapped on the floor, as though to check whether the damaged boards would hold their weight. She looked round and saw Diz's face, bright in the candlelight. That gave her some comfort. Diz smiled.

So they walked through the passageways, making detours around flaming walls and ceilings and coughing from the billows of smoke that blew into their faces every few minutes like choking fog. Sharon was sure they were being followed, but peering back over her shoulder she could see nothing. Even so, she felt certain she could hear shuffling sounds behind them. Following this creature, clinging to his gown, trying to breathe properly in the airless passageways, was making Sharon very sleepy. Her whole body ached, especially her feet and shoulders. The air was warm and stuffy. It seemed that they would never reach their destination.

But at last they did. Diz only just recognized the staffroom. The ceiling and walls were soot black and the floor was covered in fine, warm ash. The shelf was just a lump of charred wood. The armchairs looked like charcoal drawings of skeletons suspended in space, as though one breath would send them drifting away.

They crossed the room. The metal staircase was untouched by the fire, although their passing stirred soot and ash from the top few steps. Slowly they made their way down. The hooded figure before them cast great shadows on to the walls in the light from Sharon's candle.

They reached the landing and the Children could be heard behind the door that led to the cellars. There was a thump. Then another. Then muffled talking.

'They must have been there some time,' Sharon whispered. 'How do you open it?'

'Leave it for now,' Els said from behind. 'If we let them in we'll be killed in the stampede.'

They descended the second staircase. A chill breeze

blew from below, making Sharon shiver. The burning building, thought Sharon, wasn't hell. No, those old artists had been wrong. Hell was a cold, lonely place. Carefully she watched each foot as she placed it on the next step. The group continued down. They had almost reached the bottom when a sudden noise interrupted Sharon's concentration and she looked up sharply. What she saw in the room below scared her and she cried out in surprise.

The hatch to the disposal chute was wide open and standing on the other side of it, grinning, saliva dribbling from his jaws, his eyes wild with madness, was Feer. His face looked eerie in the candlelight. And in his great paws he held Alice, poised above the dank, black hole, her face pale and her eyes glazed with fright.

The party came to a sudden, jolting halt. Then Sharon's eyes fell on something that had been plain to see all along. Protruding from the folds of the robe worn by the creature who had led them there, and curling around the robe, was a long, thin, brown tail.

CHAPTER 15

WELCOME

Alice, held roughly by Feer above the open disposal chute, watched the strange, candle-lit procession come down the steps. It was led by a towering, robed creature with the head of a mouse, who was tapping on the steps with a long pole. Three children followed the creature. She recognized one as Diz, the boy they had sent her to question. She had liked him.

Alice was scared. Surely Feer wouldn't drop her? In the past she had fancied he favoured her. Even though she was really Bull's pet, Feer would often borrow her. But whether he liked her or just enjoyed annoying Bull, she didn't know. Feer had never treated her as badly as Bull did but even so, this was frightening. Her mouth was as dry as paper and she could feel herself shivering. She had never seen Feer like this, almost out of control. His grip was tight and cruel and it hurt.

Alice risked a glance into the hole below her. There was no way of knowing how far down it went – she couldn't see the bottom. If Feer dropped her, perhaps the landing would be soft. After all, they had tipped tons and tons of paper down there. But then she thought of all the other stuff that had been thrown down there in the past. She felt suddenly sick.

She found herself staring into the black emptiness and now she could make out white shapes, like huge slugs, writhing in the darkness below. She shivered and wrenched her gaze away – back to what was going on in the room.

'Put her down!' the booming voice of the mouse creature ordered Feer. 'She has never harmed you. Let her go.'

'Go away,' Feer snarled, his voice full of venom, 'or I'll drop her. Into all the loathsome muck at the bottom of the chute. The slugs can have her. I'm getting out of here as soon as the fire's out and you're not going to stop me. Now back off, or she dies.'

'Put her down,' the mouse creature repeated in a firm, calm voice, walking slowly and deliberately towards the dog and the dangling girl.

Alice could see the creature staring at Feer. There was a calmness in its eyes, a gentleness. But also great strength and a sense of power.

'The key! The key!' Diz whispered excitedly from behind Sharon. 'I can see it round his neck. I was right.'

'Back!' Feer barked, lifting Alice slightly and hugging her to him, as if to hide the key.

What can we do? Diz thought. The key, it's there. How can we get it?

'Let her go,' the mouse creature said. 'It will do you no good to drop her. Let her go, and we will deal fairly with you. Be sensible.'

146

The mouse creature was edging closer; slowly, slowly . . .

Alice felt Feer's grip tighten as he looked wildly about for some means of escape. But there was no way. Alice winced in pain.

'Back!' Feer barked again. 'I'll drop her. I mean it.'

The mouse took another step forward. Feer threw back his head, let out an ear-piercing howl – and let go of Alice.

'The crystal,' Diz yelled.

In that split second, as Alice sensed Feer's grip slacken, she felt wildly around for something to hold on to and her hand grasped the blue crystal. For a long moment Alice hung in space, dangling from the chain round Feer's neck, the crystal gripped tightly in her hand. Then she swung against the side of the hatch, the chain broke, and, still clutching the crystal, she plunged into the depths of the chute.

Diz's heart leapt as he saw Alice grab the key. But he stared in horror and dismay as he watched her hang momentarily from Feer's neck and then disappear into the hole.

Feer leapt at the robed creature, his teeth a white blur, his claws flashing. The mouse creature was ready, though. He brought his wooden pole up sharply towards Feer's face. Feer tried to twist aside in mid-flight, but the pole made contact with his nose and he fell, dazed, to the ground. Before Feer could do anything else the creature stood above him, the pole poised and ready to strike.

Feer bared his teeth. He snarled. His claws made

slashing motions in the air in a pathetic attempt to frighten the great beast that towered over him. Then he gave a feeble cry and went limp, as though his energy were draining away. He rolled on his back and lay submissive and cowering on the floor. As bullies always do, he gave in when he was beaten. 'We only wanted to go home,' he whined.

'Tie this one up!' the mouse creature commanded.

Diz remembered the rope they'd left in the big cupboard where they'd found Ginger. He opened the door. There it was. He and Moke got to work on Feer with gusto, pulling the knots tight with all their might.

Alice could feel herself falling, falling. Her breath felt as though it were being sucked from her lungs by the stale air rushing past. Then she felt strands of netting below her, curling beneath her body, and breaking her fall. She hung in space, rocking violently to and fro. Gradually the movement slowed to a gentle swaying. The stench of decay and of something worse filled her nose and her mouth. It seemed to permeate her whole body.

She could still see the hatch. It was a pale, candle-lit shape, not directly above her, but on the left. She must have rolled slightly to one side. The voice of Feer echoed faintly around and she could hear a strange humming sound somewhere below her. With one hand she felt the strands that supported her. They were thin and sticky. Spider's web? Did that mean she was safe or did it mean she was likely to be eaten? In her other hand she still held the blue crystal.

She looked down. She was close to the bottom of a vast cavern. The floor, or the layer of matter that formed the surface below her, stretched as far as she could see, in every direction. In fact, she couldn't really see the ground at all – but she could see what covered it. A carpet of white slugs, each the size of her arm, each coated in a sticky, luminous slime, writhed and twisted below her, almost within her reach. Now they were gathering at a point directly below her. They were climbing, one on top of the other, to reach her.

Alice's plight had been momentarily forgotten as the group watched Diz and Moke tie up Feer. Then Sharon stepped forward. 'Reginald, is it you?'

He turned to face her, his hood falling back to reveal his face.

'Why, of course, Sharon,' Reginald said.

Sharon ran to him and threw her arms round the big, soft, furry body beneath his cloak. Pleasure and relief ran through her. Despite everything she suddenly felt happy. Everything would be all right.

Reginald had not only grown to twice his height, but he seemed to have aged, too. His eyes had changed the most. They were clearer, more penetrating. Sharon felt as though Reginald was not only looking at her but that those eyes could somehow see through her. It was a good feeling. His gaze held kindness and compassion.

There was a noise on the staircase and they all looked up. The rest of the Brethren, led by a smiling Nigel, were descending. They had also grown.

'What happened?' Sharon asked.

'I'll tell you everything later,' Reginald replied. 'There are a few things to take care of first.'

Then Sharon remembered. Alice! She rushed across to Diz, Moke and Els who were standing at the hatch, staring gloomily down into the darkness. Diz was thinking of the key, and of the white slugs. Just when things seemed to be going right. . .

Alice watched in horror as the big white slugs reached towards her. She had to get away but couldn't move. Her body felt paralysed. But then, just as Alice thought she would be sick, she felt herself gently rising. She looked up and saw hundreds of red eyes, twinkling in the darkness like stars. She was being pulled back up to the hatch in a spider's cradle.

Children jostling. Small, tired voices cheering, yelling. Hands patting Diz, Sharon and Els, squeezing their arms. Children, standing back from the Brethren, in awe of the tall, powerful mice, the heavy hooded robes, the piercing eyes. Children, hissing, booing, kicking at Feer, the Howen leader, the cruel slave-master, being led with hanging head through the throng. Children chanting, 'We beat the Howen, we beat the Howen,' as they marched in triumphal procession to the computer room.

Alice, smiling but still shaken, with Els's arm around her, comforting her, protecting her from the bustle of excited Children.

Spiders, the Hari, crawling in their hundreds along the ceiling, safely away from the running, stamping feet of the procession, as it made its way through the dark passageways.

The Howen's reign of terror had ended. But could the last barrier be surmounted? Could they finally find their way out of this prison? Out into the blue skies of their dreams?

Diz stood before the computer, looking at the screen. The fat, blue eye looked back, the blip, like the eye's pupil, crossing the screen with regular monotony. Sharon and Els stood behind Diz, watching. Reginald stood in the safety of the doorway, still wary of the Big Cheese. The Brethren were waiting downstairs with the Children, who were still chanting, 'We beat the Howen,' while the other Rebels tried to calm them down.

Diz held the key in his right hand. He realized he was sweating, his hands hot and clammy. Was the answer really stored somewhere in this computer? They were banking on it, but they had no real reason to believe it would be there. Why should the computer solve everything? How could a computer open doors when there weren't any doors to open? Once you were in the building, escape routes seemed simply to disappear. No one – not Howen, Rebels, spiders, Brethren – had ever found any door to the outside world.

And how could the computer put out the fire that was still raging above? The fire, Diz suddenly thought, must surely have destroyed all the greyroot, by now. With no greyroot everyone would starve. And if the fire continued, surely it would burn up all the oxygen? Then they would all suffocate.

And what could the computer do about the Howen?

Now they were tied up and harmless, yes, but what next? Diz knew that neither he nor Sharon could *kill* them. He shuddered at the thought. And finally, what had made them think that the computer could send him and Sharon home? It all seemed like wishful thinking.

Still, at the very least, the computer might answer a few questions. Nervously, Diz held the prism of blue crystal above the triangular hole and let it go. It slid into the hole with a soft click. A perfect fit!

The blip travelled across the screen for one last time and disappeared off the edge. A cursor flashed in the top left-hand corner of the three-sided screen. Diz felt a little thrill of pleasure, mingled with relief. Gingerly he tapped a key, half expecting to get an electric shock. Nothing happened. So far so good. He found the letters on the keyboard for HELLO and tapped them in. Nothing. He tried what looked like the return key. A row of letters and symbols appeared on the screen, but they made no sense at all.

He tried again. He typed in his name, the names of Sharon, Els, Moke, Alice, Ginger, the Brethren, the Howen ... He typed in words of greeting. Hello. How do you do? Wakey Wakey. Is there anybody there? I'm a little teapot, short and stout, here's my handle, here's my spout ... Each time the computer responded with words or sentences in gibberish.

Diz tried a few other keys, those marked with strange symbols. Nothing. Then he tried different combinations of keys. His earlier pessimism was returning. What did they expect, really? He stared disconsolately at the keys with unusual symbols, wondering what they could mean. He and the others had defeated the Howen. They had activated the computer. But they were still trapped, perhaps for ever. Diz felt tears welling up. Were they really beaten? No, he was *not* going to give up. He tried more words. He tried combinations of keys. He tried everything he could think of while behind him Sharon waited patiently, occasionally murmuring words of encouragement.

In desperation he typed in HELP. The computer made a bleeping sound. A word appeared on the screen that Diz and Sharon recognized. Diz threw his hands in the air and cheered. He looked round at Sharon. She was grinning.

The word said WELCOME.

'OK,' Diz said. 'Any bright ideas what to do next?'

'Try Menu,' Sharon suggested. Diz typed it in. M - E - N - U. A list of options came up on the screen.

A LIFE-SUPPORT SYSTEMS
B COMMUNICATION
C MAINTENANCE
D REPAIR SYSTEMS
E MENU 2

'Which one?' Diz asked.

'Try the first one.'

Diz pressed the letter A followed by the return key. Rows of meaningless figures scrolled up the screen. Then the screen cleared, leaving the words MEMORY IN TURMOIL flashing.

'Great,' groaned Diz. 'What on earth does that mean?'

'Try REPAIR SYSTEMS. It might be a simple fault that we can mend.'

Diz pressed the D and then the return key.

ACTIVATE SYSTEMS?

Diz typed in YES.

OK, the computer said.

'That's more hopeful,' Sharon said.

'What now?' Diz asked.

'Try asking it some questions,' suggested Reginald, who, caught up in the excitement, had conquered his wariness of the strange machine, and was now standing behind them.

'Perhaps we use COMMUNICATION for that,' Diz said, and keyed in B. The screen cleared and the cursor flashed.

Diz typed in – HOW DO WE GET HOME?

MORE INFORMATION PLEASE, the computer responded.

Diz started typing in information. Who he was. Who Sharon was. Where they lived – the town, the country, the planet, the star they circled, although all he could think to call it was the sun. He typed in facts about his school and about the DT storeroom and he told the computer how they had arrived in the building.

'Here goes, then,' he said anxiously, and he lightly tapped the return key.

They all stared expectantly at the blank screen. Long, long seconds passed before the screen came to life.

YOU WISH TO UNLOCK THE DOOR TO YOUR WORLD?

'Put yes,' Sharon said excitedly.

'All right, all right.' Diz typed it in.

Again they waited, staring at the screen. At last one word appeared, glowing on the pale-blue screen.

UNLOCKED

'Is that it, then?' Diz asked.

'It means we can go home,' Sharon cried, and squeezed his shoulders.

'Let's just try the menu again,' Diz said.

The menu came up on the screen and they stared at the categories. Diz tried C for Maintenance. After much meaningless scrolling the computer finally said MEMORY BEWILDERED.

Then Diz tried E for the second menu. This time it said ENTER PASSWORD.

'That's it, then,' Diz said. 'We'll never work that out. Not in a million years.'

At that moment Moke burst into the room. 'There's water everywhere,' he panted. 'The whole place is flooding. Water's pouring down the main staircase. And there's steam. Not smoke, steam! The fire's going out.'

'Wonderful,' Diz cried. 'The computer *has* activated the repair systems.'

The Hari floated down from the ceiling on a fine, silver thread, and landed without a sound on the edge of the computer.

Now work the Spinner for Hari, the spider said. *It must open our door, too.*

Diz entered the information as the Hari gave it. It was a confusing mass of signs and symbols. So were the replies. He could make no sense of it. But he owed the Hari this. He pressed the return key. Strange symbols flashed on to the screen.

It is done. Now give me your hand, the Hari said to Diz. He held it out, his childhood fear conquered, and the spider climbed on to it, and up on to Diz's shoulder.

Take me into the next room, the Hari said.

Diz walked slowly into the hallway. The others followed close behind. The door to the as-yet-unexplored room was open. Diz gasped. The room was crawling with spiders, more than he had ever seen in his life. They covered the walls like furry, moving wallpaper and formed a thick carpet of bodies and legs on the floor.

On the far wall, a light began to glow. At first it looked as though a spotlight were being shone on it, like a projector before the first slide is shown. Then the circle of light grew brighter, and brighter still, until it shone with the ferocity of a sun. They could only look at it by shielding their eyes with their hands.

But the circle of light also had depth. Now they could see it was really a hole in the wall, with the blinding light shining from beyond. It was a tunnel, going on for ever into the brightness. A glowing tunnel, stretching to infinity. The light dimmed slightly and the onlookers could just make out a glittering mass of silver strands lining the tunnel. The tunnel was a web.

Farewell, the Hari said. But not with one voice. This time there were hundreds of voices, all speaking in unison. A full, rich, warm, many-layered goodbye.

We think we will meet again, the voices said. *Until*

then, we thank you. We had nearly worked it out. You were the last piece in the puzzle. Goodspin.

The spiders began to move. Slowly at first, but then gaining in speed, they filed over the edge of the hole into the brilliant webbed tunnel, a stream of black silhouettes against the bright light. They were going home.

Fascinated, the group watched the spiders leave. After several minutes the last spider, the one on Diz's shoulder, passed into the hole. (Was that the spider who had freed him in the staffroom? Diz wondered.) Then the light faded and they were all staring at a blank wall in an empty room.

Diz blinked several times, trying to clear the great, purple after-image that was bouncing around in front of his vision.

'Goodbye Hari,' he said softly, 'and goodspin.'

Reginald and the Brethren stood before Diz, Sharon and the Rebels in the cellars below the office stairs. The light from several candles, lit from the dying torches, flickered around them. Reginald held Diz's and Sharon's hands.

'You two must go now,' he said.

'But what about you?' Sharon asked in alarm.

'We have made our Change,' Reginald replied. 'The Game of Changes has been won. We made the final move and it was the right one. We have been transformed by fire.' He paused for a moment and smiled. 'Does your race not undergo a transformation? Do you not leave your childish ways and become adults, to act as guardians of your world, to care for it? Do you not become mature?'

'We grow up, I suppose,' Sharon said, thinking back to their earlier conversation. How long ago it seemed now. She thought of the way most adults treated their world. They could hardly be said to care for it.

Reginald continued. 'The fire has transformed us and I believe we can now operate the Big Cheese.' He chuckled. 'This building is more than just a building. It is a giant trap. Why it should be so, and what evil beings built it, we do not know. But we understand two things: those who built it are no longer here and the building is damaged in some way. However, thanks to you, Diz and Sharon, we can open the doors. We can free the Children. We can even return the Howen to their own land. But for how long the doors will remain open we do not know. If the building is damaged the balance of power may not hold for long. You must go quickly, before the door to your world closes again.'

'But what about you?' Sharon asked again.

'Don't worry. We will find the door to our own land, too. And we will look after the Children. We will make sure they find their way safely. Now go.'

'Will you really free the Howen?' Diz questioned.

'Yes.' Reginald smiled grimly. 'They must go home, too. Perhaps this experience will make them kinder. Perhaps not. It is not for us to judge.'

Diz remembered Feer's eyes in that unguarded moment, that desperately lost and sad look. 'You're right,' he said.

'Will we ever see you again?' Sharon asked.

'Questions, questions, questions. Who knows where our paths will lead us.'

Sharon pulled the red handkerchief from her pocket.

'Here. I found this,' she said. 'You'd better have it back.'

'You may keep it, if you like. I don't need it any more.'

'Because you are the Abbot?'

'Goodness, no,' Reginald laughed. 'Being the Abbot was just a childhood game.'

'I liked your pointy hat really,' Sharon said.

Reginald smiled. Then Sharon turned to Els and the Rebels who had gathered around. 'I hope everything goes all right and you find your way home.'

'I'm going to find my mum,' Jaro said, and Bel squeezed his hand. Everyone smiled but Els. She could still remember the fighting, the war that was waging when they had been taken to the building because then everyone had thought it was a safe place to hide. She remembered blood and the pain in people's eyes. When they returned home, what would they find? Would their homes still be there? Would their parents still be alive? But she said nothing, for this was a time of joy. She would not spoil the mood. She stepped forward and kissed Sharon and Diz awkwardly.

'Thank you,' she said. 'Perhaps we'll see you again one day.'

'Good luck, then,' Diz said, a little embarrassed by the kiss.

'Just think,' Baloney piped up. 'We'll be able to eat real food again.' He was chewing a piece of blackened greyroot.

'What's that?' asked Diz.

'Greyroot from the fire,' Baloney said. 'The heat has changed it, made it softer.'

'It's cooked,' Diz said. 'Does it taste any better?'

'No,' Baloney replied.

'I didn't think it would,' Diz said, and they all laughed.

The laughter died and they were all quiet for a few moments. 'Goodbye everyone,' Sharon finally said, breaking the silence, a lump in her throat and a prickling in her eyes. She didn't want to cry but she couldn't stop the tear that rolled down her cheek. She turned to Reginald and held out her hand.

The great mouse stared at it solemnly.

'You're supposed to shake it,' Els said.

'I don't know whether I feel happy or sad,' Sharon said to Diz as they walked hurriedly through the underground passages towards the main staircase. They had just made a complicated detour around a pool of water that filled the passage like an underground lake. Sharon led the way with the torch they'd recovered from Feer. Its beam was very weak. Diz had Raffer's bone as a souvenir. He clicked it along the wall as they jogged down the passage.

'I know what you mean,' Diz agreed. 'They are our friends, aren't they? Moke, Els, little Crab, all the others. Even Ginger, in his way.'

'Goodbyes *are* sad,' Sharon said. 'But we'll be home soon.'

Then they became aware of the sound. It had been going on for some time, quietly, in the background.

Now they heard it loud and clear, getting closer. A powerful, high-pitched whine.

'Don't speak too soon,' Diz muttered, stopping in his tracks. 'We're not home yet.'

The torch gave its last glimmer of light and went out.

CHAPTER 16

DOG-TIRED

The great body of the Prowler lumbered towards them. Its eye glowed brightly, lighting up the passageway. Its armour shone. Its great, tentacle-like arms hovered in front, scraping back and forth across the walls and ceilings. Its high-pitched whine filled their ears.

Diz glanced at Sharon in alarm.

'The Prowler,' she said, grinning. 'I knew it was a robot all along but I didn't think –' She burst into helpless laughter.

'So that's the Prowler.' Diz laughed, too. Sharon's giggles were infectious.

The great vacuum-cleaning robot trundled towards them, its tubes sucking up dust and dirt from the nooks and crannies of the passage, while rubbish from the floor was whirled away as it passed over. It was fully operational again; the computer had repaired every part of the system. The machine's eye scanned ahead and its brush attachments whirled merrily. Without a second glance, it carefully passed Diz and Sharon, who huddled against the wall, and disappeared behind them in a pool of light.

Sharon and Diz had reached the top of the main staircase when the lights came back on. Amazing, Diz thought. Whatever could they be made of to withstand the heat of that fire? They walked quickly through the puddles of water towards the room where they had first sighted the Howen all that time ago. They hurried because they'd suddenly remembered Reginald's warning. If the door to their world closed . . . The door to their world? This building had doors to so many other dimensions . . .

They made their way partly from memory, partly from the directions Reginald had given them. Left, right, second left . . . The floors were awash. Half-burnt beams and wooden panels floated in pools of water. And where water had washed the soot and burnt wood away from the walls and ceilings, they could see metal. Blackened and scorched, but metal none the less.

'Did Reginald mean this building's a spaceship, then?' Sharon asked Diz.

'None of the walls are actually damaged, are they?' Diz replied. 'All the wood, the school bits, they just seem to be stuck on, not part of the real building. They're the bits that have burned, not the metal underneath.'

'But why dress the place up as a school?'

'To disguise it?' suggested Diz. 'To camouflage it? To turn it into a trap?'

'But who would go to all that trouble? And why? Was the trap for us, or did we just stumble into it by accident? You know, like the way little animals crawl into bottles left lying around in fields and can't get out again.'

'I don't know,' Diz said. 'I'll just be pleased to see the back of it.'

'Perhaps it's a time machine, like Doctor Who's Tardis.'

'I thought of that, too. But it doesn't really explain much, does it?'

At last they reached the classroom that led to the attic, the room where they had first seen the Howen.

'Well, I never,' Diz laughed. Hanging from the trapdoor was a rope ladder. 'I wondered how we were going to get back up there. The Brethren must have left it for us.'

At that moment the building seemed to lurch. The floor shifted slightly and for a moment Diz and Sharon lost their balance.

'What was that?' Diz gasped.

'Reginald said the building was damaged,' Sharon said. 'It must be falling apart. Maybe the fire and getting the computer working again was too much for it. We'd better hurry.'

'Or if it is a spaceship, perhaps it's going to take off!'

Quickly they clambered up the ladder and were soon picking their way back over the joists, walking carefully in the darkness of the attic.

'It's this way, I think,' Sharon whispered.

'Could any of the Howen have found their way back into our world?' Diz asked.

'No, I'm pretty sure the door closed behind us as soon as we arrived,' Sharon said. 'The Brethren helped me search but there was no sign of it.'

Diz thought back to the feeling he'd had after they had first climbed the wall and shuddered. He realized that he had known then that they were trapped. Would the wall be there now? And would it be low enough to climb over?

They made their way on in the darkness as fast as they could.

'What day is it?' Diz asked.

'It must be Saturday,' Sharon replied. 'Mum'll be frantic.'

'I'm starving.'

'And I feel filthy. I can't wait for a shower.'

'Oh, I can,' Diz said.

At last they found it. The wall was ahead of them in the darkness. And it did not reach up out of sight. With great relief they helped one another to scramble over it, letting themselves down carefully on to the box they'd left on the other side. As they climbed, Diz was careful not to damage his precious souvenir, Raffer's bone.

The trapdoor down to the storeroom was still open, as they'd left it.

'What's that noise?' Diz hissed. 'Listen!'

They could hear the moan of the wind blowing around the attic. But above the noise of the wind was the unmistakable sound of a dog barking.

Sharon let herself down on to the stepladder into the storeroom. Awkwardly Diz followed her, closing the trapdoor above him. Then he moved the ladder and leaned it against the wall. Nothing seemed to have changed; it all looked as they'd left it. But on the other side of the door, a dog was barking excitedly.

They heard the key turn in the lock and the door jerked open. An Alsatian peered round and barked once. The dog's head was followed by that of a policeman. He gave them a very serious look, and then he smiled.

'It's all right,' the policeman said. Then his head disappeared and they heard him shouting. 'We've found them. They're safe.'

Diz realized he was still holding Raffer's bone. How would he explain that? He quickly pushed it behind a pile of wood. No one would ever notice it among the junk. He'd collect it next week.

Diz and Sharon emerged from the DT room into the last light of day. Saturday evening was giving way to night. A gale was blowing. The bright orange tape that surrounded the condemned part of the building was flapping wildly in the wind. Leaves and empty crisp packets chased madly around the playground, now littered with broken roof tiles. The two children could hardly believe they were safe at last. Diz looked up and saw the magpie, now joined by a second – his mate, perhaps – perched on the clock tower. Then the birds were gone, whisked away by the gale. The school clock said twenty past something as always and was it his imagination or did he see the clock tower sway in the wind? Would the clock tower last the night? Their mother was rushing towards them, wailing, her arms outstretched. Their father stood to one side, his hand rubbing his eyes as though he were tired. Diz and Sharon knew they were going to cry, too.

The policeman took Diz, Sharon and their mother home in his car. Diz thought he had never felt so weary. Every part of his body seemed to be aching. Soon there would be food and a warm, cosy bed. Explanations could wait until morning.

Sharon felt for the red handkerchief in her pocket and smiled to herself. She was tired out, too.

'Look,' Diz whispered, pointing out of the window. 'See that star, all on its own. Do you know its name?' A star shone brightly in a patch of sky, momentarily clear of the rushing black clouds.

'The Dog Star?' Sharon asked, and they both started giggling.

'I didn't know you knew anything about astronomy,' their mum said, putting an arm round each of them protectively.

In the storeroom the light had been left on. The trapdoor creaked, and opened. Several pieces of shaped wood fell through and clattered on to the floor. These were followed by a wooden board – the Game of Changes. Then two legs appeared. Soon a boy hung from the wooden frame, judging the distance to the ground.

Ginger dropped and landed lightly, safely. He gathered the pieces of the game together and straightened up. He grasped the handle of the storeroom door. What strange and unknown land was he about to encounter on the other side?